'I still say you should never have given him tools, Number 2. Any tool magnifies his ability to do things. And he does enough bare-handed –'

'Number 4, what he does is all we can monitor. The less he does, the more I would worry. For over a year he brooded, and continually attempted to escape.

'You see, he has never had any reason to *want* to stay here. The Village is a beautiful place; it is Shangri-La by the seashore. But a certain personality type, with nothing to do, will go to amazing lengths to find a direction for his energies. I'm simply channelling his drive into paths we can observe.'

'Don't underestimate him, Number 2. And don't over-estimate yourself . . .'

Dedicated with admiration to Dan Curtis,
and with awe to Art Wallace.

The prisoner
Who is No. 2 ?

DAVID McDANIEL

BOXTREE

Published by the UK 1992
by BOXTREE LIMITED
Broadwall House
21 Broadwall
London SE1 9PL

First published in the USA 1970 by Ace Books

First published in Great Britain 1979 by
Dobson Books Ltd

First New English Library Paperback Edition April 1981
published by New English Library Ltd.

10 9 8 7 6 5 4 3 2 1

Cover photograph courtesy of ITC Entertainment Group Ltd.

Cover design by Head

Typeset by DP Photosetting, Aylesbury, Bucks.

Printed and bound by Cox & Wyman Ltd., Reading, Berkshire

1-85283-830-2

A catalogue record for this book is available from the
British Library

Contents

Section I: Introduction

Drake woke. Automatically, naturally, without an alarm, he came to consciousness. London muttered outside his windows in the bright morning as he stretched, slowly, luxuriously, fitting every joint comfortably into place, feeling his body from the bones outward to the soft rumpled ridges of the sheets against his skin.

It was a matter of thirty seconds before he finished flushing his lungs with a yawn, and then he was out of bed padding barefoot to the bathroom and pulling on a robe. His shower was brief and brisk, scouring the last of sleep's residue from his skin and followed by a great rough shaggy towel which wrapped him while he shaved.

Outside the tall front windows his hand-built pet, his long low lovely green KAR 1260, crouched in the 8.00 A.M. sunshine of Upper Berkeley Mews. Such an exceptionally fine day as this deserved to be driven through. *Bristol*? he asked himself as he lit the gas under a kettle and removed three eggs from the fridge. *King's Lynn*?

He started a pan of water heating and returned to his room. He dressed casually, in layers, with the possibility in mind that it might actually get warm later. Over a V-necked sweater he chose to wear a jacket.

He picked one from his closet where it hung with the rest – a nicely-cut navy blue blazer with white piping and a few nearly imperceptible pinholes in the left lapel. He slipped it from the hanger where it waited his pleasure.

This badgeless blazer was his reminder; though he wore no number, a few hundred forgotten men and women did. But for today, it was not a flag of revolution but a comfortable coat for a drive to Cheltenham or Lincoln.

His kettle spluttered wetly for a moment, chirped, twittered, and began to build to a piercing whistle before he came in to remove it from the gas and pour from it into a waiting cup. He sluiced the water around the inside of the china bowl, then dumped it thriftily back in the kettle. The tea-strainer lay filled and ready; he dropped it into the heated cup and poured the seething water over it.

A long keen knife divided a lemon from the cooler; half was dropped into the cup to steep with the tea and half was pressed into a plastic film which would preserve its freshness for half an hour.

He glanced at his wrist-chronometer as he slipped the three eggs into the pan of bubbling water and reduced the gas flame, then plucked three lumps of sugar from a bowl on the first shelf and dropped them into the darkening tea.

Satisfied with its colour, he lifted out the tea-strainer and the steaming lemon and carried the cup with him back into the sitting room. He sipped at it as he sorted happily through a stack of county ordnance maps, considering a day's drive to Coventry, or a night at St. Ives.

Another glance at his wristwatch sent him back to start two slices of bread toasting while his plate warmed under the same electric coils for two minutes. When the unit switched off, he had thirty seconds before his eggs were ready – just long enough to arrange the toast tastefully and pass a light coat of butter across it.

While his eggs, opened, approached eating temperature, he made a second cup of tea. Then he dusted the firm, opaque whites and glossy liquid yolks with a sprinkling of salt and a few twists of white pepper from the grinder. He used the second lemon half, dropped in two lumps of sugar and sat down to breakfast.

It was well past the half-hour when he put the last of his utensils away, secured the kitchen and prepared to leave. A hat, a driving scarf, his gloves, his blazer and the map of Norfolk. His currency case and his keys. Then down the short, carpeted front hall to the outside door, past the closed and silent doors of two adjoining flats, to the heavy metal knob which turned beneath his hand and which he drew toward him as he had done every morning he'd been home for the last five years. Outside, a short flight of cement steps led down to the narrow pavement and his car, and faceless blocks of flats stretched to both ends of the street.

But this morning they didn't.

Outside his door, of his flat, in London, the ground was level with a single step to the doorstep and a neatly bordered path with flowering rows ran along the front of his solitary building. The air was crisp and salty. Across green lawns early-blooming beds of spring flowers were a riot of glorious colour, and low rough-stone walls behind them held back a grassy slope decorated with cosily quaint buildings. Above them all rose a more massive structure with an eye-catching green dome.

He looked down. About waist height, just to the left of his door, so mounted as to be easily seen from either direction, a sign hung from a white post with a posy of nearly-fresh flowers nodding from the planter in its top.

The sign said simply, '6'.

*

He started from the impossible and worked his way back. The outside of the door itself was the right colour, and the latch was correct. There was no lock. He tried the door of the first apartment – the knob spun loosely, but the wooden panel affixed to the wall like an imitation door (non-practical) in a stage set had neither hinges, jamb, nor any room behind it.

He stood in the hall a moment, then looked back into his flat. It was the same – it was his London flat, where he had gone to sleep last night, where he awakened this morning, breakfasted on eggs he had bought yesterday in Covent Garden, and through the windows of which he had just looked at the street and his KAR.

He returned to the windows and stared out of them at the same scene. The street was still there, and his green racing car still waited at the kerb below. And yet, somehow, with the image of grass and flowers, and gravelled walks and a shining green dome still in his mind's eye as he examined the scene, some quality, almost imperceptibly, seemed to be missing from it. The street seemed uncommonly still, and was there a trace of unsteadiness about that walking figure . . .?

An eerie silence spread from nowhere, as if a giant hand were wrapping sheets of cotton around the entire flat. The almost-unheard noises of the city faded, and were gone. In the sudden dense stillness, a voice spoke behind him.

'It's a holographic projection, Number 6. Rather nice, don't you think?' The voice was unfamiliar – a sharp, grating voice with a raucous edge to it.

Slowly he turned. The screen of his television set, a commonplace commercial model, was aglow. As he watched, the face of a stranger appeared on the screen, with intent eyes and a quick, glittering smile.

'Welcome back, Number 6. Can you see me all right now? Good.'

'Who are you?'

'The new Number 2. I'm afraid the Village just couldn't get along without you when you walked off the job, so you have regretfully been removed from your position of responsibility and restored to your old status. I was asked to replace you. In view of the revised situation, I suggest you consider the words of the great English poet who wrote, "*Now that I'm Six, I'm as clever as clever – so I think I'll be Six for ever and ever.*"'

He walked to the television controls and switched to BBC-2. The picture did not change.

'Sorry, Number 6; you'll find I'm on all the channels. Your brief tenure as Number 2 was certainly one of the most . . . active on record, but it did very little towards ensuring the mutuality of the Village. And this, after all, is the first responsibility of Number 2.

'Now,' he continued, 'there are probably a number of things you haven't really understood. If you have any questions . . .?'

'Could I believe your answers?'

'You are welcome to – in fact, you are invited to. Let me see . . . *your* predecessor as Number 2 had "Granny Bug" designed and programmed – an exquisite job – not exactly robotic, she was more in the nature of a cyborg, if you know the term. In fact, she was human, as far as she went. But after you left us she proved not to be worth repairing and was salvaged for parts, since a good deal of expense had gone into her in the first place.'

'All that just to fool me! I'm retroactively honoured.'

'Not all for you, Number 6. You're important, but not *that* important. No, Granny's main duty was observation. That particular Number 2 had a deep inner drive for covertitude, if I may coin a term – one which I do not share. All this hiding around corners, spying on one's friends and fellow-Villagers – it's distasteful to me.'

Slowly and deliberately, the man who was now called Number 6 walked back across the room and sat down. As an afterthought, he removed the map of Norfolk from his pocket and tossed it on the table. His eyes flicked around the room . . . *his* room – back to the unfamiliar gentleman on the telly – into the kitchenette – out of the window to the tops of *(nonexistent?)* blocks of flats across the street – searching for something he'd missed that could have warned him of the miraculous transportation that had taken place while he slept. As he looked, the background track faded quietly up to its natural level, and with the sound of distant traffic he was almost back in London. Now he was aware of the difference that had completely escaped him. It didn't smell like London – but he hadn't noticed.

'You seem to have gone to some expense redecorating while I was away.'

'We wanted you to feel at home, Number 6. You are a valuable individual; your well-being is of very real concern to us. This careful reconstruction of your natural habitat has been provided for your personal comfort. It took quite a while to prepare, too. The efforts of many people have gone into making this home-from-home ready for you.'

'So I'm an individual now. But my name is not "Number 6."'

'Number 6, the Village exists only to serve you – and others like you. Our facilities are sophisticated, but not unlimited. We have enough work to do that clumsy, irregular things like names only serve to get in the way. One can handle people so much more efficiently by numbers, and thereby do more for more people. After all, isn't one set of symbols as good as another for representing yourself as long as everyone is agreed it's you?'

'Not to me. I want to decide my own arbitrary set of symbols, not be forced to accept someone else's.'

'Come now. Your parents named you – you didn't choose your name.'

'I could have.'

'You argue like a Scot. I will not be drawn into a debate with you. I hate debates – they turn a conversation into a contest.' Number 2 looked off to one side and nodded, then smiled brightly out of the screen. 'Now you see what happens when I let you monopolise the conversation – your welcome isn't even completed yet.'

Just outside the back door of the flat, a door which opened from a small porch beyond the kitchenette into a dingy airshaft which connected to an alley through a narrow passageway, an electric starter whined briefly and a powerful internal combustion engine fired, coughed, fired again and caught, then speeded up to a stuttering roar filled with misfires for several seconds before slowing to an idle.

'If you will look outside your back door, I think you will find a most pleasant surprise.'

Reluctantly, Number 6 rose from his chair and walked back through the dining area, through the kitchenette, and through the porch.

Outside the back door it was spring. Bright sunshine dappled warmly over tall flowers on either side of the door, and a single cement step lay between the doorsill and the bare dirt floor of a simple open-ended lean-to shelter which stood against the side of the building. From the outside, the main structure didn't look any different from the Basic Cottage Unit he had occupied during what he liked to think of as his previous visits to the Village. Which meant only the interior had been modified, and since the room plan was different, this left a fair amount of space here and there between outer and inner walls. Doubtless it had not been allowed to go to waste; he filed the observation.

The three walls of the shed bore waist-high work-benches, electric sockets and assorted shelves. Two or three doors were artfully ajar, and he could see tools neatly arrayed behind them – likely his own personally collected, carefully selected set, or another so similar he would be unable to tell the difference.

And in the centre of the shed, nearly filling it, stood KAR 1260; idling, and missing badly. The key stood from the ignition lock, waiting for him to accept the reality before him.

'It sounds as if it needs a little work, Number 6. You've been away from it for quite a while, you know.' Number 2's cheerful face looked down at him from a standard Village monitor above the shelves to his right.

The engine needed tuning at least, and something was odd about the fuel flow – it would need work, as Number 2 said. So they were not only willing to give him special consideration to the extent of a custom dwelling, but they were giving him something to occupy his idle time. If he was willing to accept it.

Not only that, but it could be expected to serve as a hostage. The machine mattered more to him than any living human – and would be harder to take with him in another escape attempt.

Someone else had started it – he could refuse to accept the responsibility for it, leaving it to idle here for a few hours until it ran out of fuel and stopped naturally, and then avoiding the use of his back door entirely until they tired of the game and took it away. He could. He looked at it for a minute and more, listening to the uncomfortable sound of an engine which needed work – his engine.

Finally, resolutely, he reached forward and shut off the ignition. It was still his car, and even here in the Village he was glad to have it with him. He touched the wheel lightly with his fingertips and ran his eyes over the shining instrumentation and the deep curve of the leather driver's seat. This wasn't a duplicate – not even a perfect duplicate. There was something of himself in this machine, and he could sense it. This was his.

'It's a lovely car,' said Number 2's faintly raucous voice. 'I don't wonder that you missed it while you were here before – it's almost an extension of yourself.'

They seemed to be intent on making his existence satisfactory here, and it was annoying to realise they were making progress. But for the fact that what he demanded was the one thing they could not give him, he was almost ready to admit (but only to himself) that they might succeed.

'Why, who knows, Number 6! You might even come to like it here.'

'As the Bishop said to the Actress. I don't recall seeing a source of petrol around the Village – has that been changed as well?'

'That may prove a difficulty,' said Number 2 regretfully. 'We could have adapted your car to a nuclear-fusion engine, but that would hardly allow you of much tinkering. They can be monstrously tricky. Still, we can doubtless find you a few gallons from time to time; either the chemist's or the ironmonger's might carry the necessary forms. There may be a scarcity – I suggest you look upon it as an incentive to improve your carburation.

'There have been those around me who have disapproved of allowing you to have access to tools, by the way – they feel you are not to be trusted under any circumstances. I really hope you won't bear them out.'

'It would be too much to ask for a road to drive on.'

'My dear Number 6! This long-ton of metal was brought here with great difficulty, at tremendous expense, and by helicopter – a truly impressive sight, I must say – especially for you. I quite understand the frustrations such a situation might engender, but you must appreciate the limited space with which we have to work. The impossible is simple; the inconceivable may take some thinking. You'd best see to that engine before you think about racing. I expect you'll find the altitude necessitates careful tuning and adjustment.' He paused. 'Then if you have no more questions at the moment, you may have some later. After you're re-oriented to the Village, perhaps you would join me for lunch tomorrow, if you're free.'

'I don't expect to be called away suddenly.'

'Quite right. We try to avoid such emergencies in the Village. Be seeing you.'

The screen faded, and in the silence he could hear the familiar sound of breakers stroking a sandy beach just beyond the cliff edge. Back inside the cottage was his flat in London, as real and cosy and warm as he had formed it around his own tastes, prejudices and idiosyncrasies over five years. He had his own home, fitted around his personality like a well-worn shoe; he had his own creation, KAR 1260; he had his tools. And in the inviolate privacy of his own mind, he admitted Number 2's advisers were correct. He couldn't be trusted with tools, and his only remaining uncertainty was how far away he would be before this truth was acknowledged by Number 2.

Far behind his lips he smiled the slow secret smile of confidence challenged, and prepared to begin.

Section II: Allegro

He walked whistling up the front steps to the big bronze doors at the foot of the green-domed building on the hill. If anyone recognised the melody, they made no sign.

Singing toorali – oorali – addie,
Singing toorali – ooraliay;
Singing toorali – oorali – addie,
And I'll see you in Botany Bay!

That was how the refrain would have run if anyone had cared to sing it at this time, in this place; it was a song of ancient and dishonourable heritage, its wryly cheerful melody wrought by men a century dead, imprisoned and exiled.

The bronze doors gave back before him as he set foot on the porch and entered an elegantly empty hall. The sunlight and quiet sounds of the Village damped behind him as the outer doors closed silently and the inner doors opened into what could have been a film set for an imaginative control centre. A round room, like a planetarium dome with a sunken floor, panelled with moving images, realistic and abstract, flickering like an electron shell around the circular, instrumented desk and the spherical rotating chair – the nucleus of this gigantic atom into which, like some unnamed particle with no particular charge or mass and undetermined potential energy, he had wandered.

At the focus of this concentration of power, in the cradle of the chair, sat Number 2. He was slighter of build than he had seemed by television, with black hair and eyes that pierced like his voice. He looked up as his guest entered and a chair by the desk rose smoothly from the floor for him.

'You're not wearing your pin, Number 6. Don't you want people to know who you are?'

'Not particularly, since I don't particularly care to know who *they* are. If I want to know I can ask.'

'But consider – suppose a fellow Villager wanted to invite you for a glass of wine, but didn't know how to introduce you to his friend, the waiter. It would be socially embarrassing for him.'

'I don't usually drink with strangers.'

'You do when it suits your purpose,' Number 2 said blithely. 'But fortunately, you and I know each other. Hence I have invited you for lunch – and you have accepted.'

Two bowls of soup rose from a sliding panel in the desk between them, complete with napkins and spoons, as Number 2 continued to press his point. 'If I saw a tree falling towards you, what would I shout to warn you? More practically, if it is your turn to be helped in a shop, isn't it simpler if the assistant can say, "You're next, Number 6," instead of "You without the pin."'

'Since you brought that up, Number 2 – just whom do I see about petrol?'

'Is your engine retuned already? It sounded as if restoring it to operative efficiency would be quite a lengthy affair.'

'From what you'd implied, I'd gathered it might take a while to find something to run it on. So I thought to start searching. Where should I inquire?'

'I'm not really sure what department that would be under. Surely it's listed somewhere, but I was waiting until you were ready to detail your requirements. What kind of fuel did you want, and how much? More than a few gallons will require special shipment, so we may as well ask for the best.'

'Any lead-free anti-knock motor petrol with an octane rating around one hundred and thirty would be more than satisfactory. I'll want at least twenty gallons for the adjustment work – I can't very well tune an engine that won't run.'

'Well, let's see, Number 6. The chemist's could probably help you with a litre or two – the art supply shop might carry something similar as well, come to think of it. The ironmonger might be able to order some – he has the proper storage facilities as well. I suppose I'll have to look this up somewhere. Could we table this for a day?'

'It's in your hands.'

'Yes – everything is. It's really tiresome, sometimes. I see you enjoyed the soup. Do have a lamb sandwich . . .

'Suppose I had a butler. He wouldn't know how to introduce you, since calling cards are out of fashion.'

'So are butlers – even short silent ones.'

'Seriously, Number 6, I'm trying to explain why it is important you wear your Number. Be proud of your identity. Or do you prefer the notoriety of being known as The Man Without A Pin?'

'As long as I'm the only one around and it's perfectly clear who they're referring to, it's as good a name as any other. It may be a little long, but it's my own name, earned and not assigned. Besides, I shouldn't like seeing my name constantly repeated in telephone numbers and lorry licences.'

'Your parents named you arbitrarily, Number 6 – we have only re-named you as part of our family. We covered this particular chain of argument yesterday. Suppose more people started going around without Numbers – then no one could be sure who *the man without a pin* was. What would you do then? Carry a walking stick? Wear a red coat, or a flower? Cultivate a moustache? Don't you see that it is in everyone's best interests that we all agree on who we are in such a way that there is a minimum possibility of confusion? Any symbols could be picked and ordered, but they must be specific. Numbers are the easiest to handle, the most efficient. That's all. I don't want you to start arguing relative morality now – we simply cannot change the entire Village to suit your whim. You may call yourself what you like, but your accounts are kept as Number 6, your medical and credit information as well; and to us in the Village you will always be known, simply, as Number 6.

'Now why not wear your pin, like a good fellow? I

certainly hope I won't have occasion to bring this up again. now, the Village Entertainment Committee has organised a small group doing Gilbert and Sullivan –'

'*Yeoman of the Guard?*'

'Your favourite? No – I believe the production will be more appropriate. *Patience*. They've found a most talented soprano and an acceptable organist. Or do your tastes run more to Shakespeare and the Greeks? You should involve yourself in lighter things, Number 6. Take up a hobby. Don't just pace up and down your cage.'

*

Some three hours past his own breakfast the following morning, Number 6 called at the small hardware store in the Village. As the bell above the door tinkled to announce his entry, the sturdy shopkeeper looked up behind the counter.

'Good morning, Number – ah . . .'

'Good morning, Number 26. I was wondering if you might have a few gallons of petrol about the place. Number 2 suggested I ask here.'

'Oh, Number 6!' He put down a sheaf of stapled pages and rose. 'Yes, of course. Number 2 told me you might be coming in.'

He seemed so willing to help that his customer was taken slightly aback. Was it possible that it could be this simple? Of course not.

'You'll need three copies of Form 739/H-F – that's *hydrocarbon, fuel,* I think. There isn't anything that needs to be approved, though – no red tape to worry about. Just for the records.'

'How much can I get?'

Number 26 shrugged. 'I wouldn't have a guess. We usually stock the forms, but nobody's ever asked for more than a gallon at a time. It'd depend on how much was available, I suppose. How much did you plan on asking for?'

'I could easily use fifty gallons, and one hundred would not be too much.'

'My word! Where would keep all that petrol? And what on earth would you do with it?'

'Didn't Number 2 tell you? I have an eight-cylinder engine to feed. As for storage, I was hoping you could tell me.'

'Well, it's not a problem that's come up before. I suppose you'll want a tank of some kind, probably with a hose. The Safety Committee will want to approve the arrangement anyway – they'll be happy to help you in whatever way they can. Don't want your home to burn down in the middle of the night, after all.' He paused and scratched his head. 'You'll probably want to file an 8704/S – that's clearance for storage of dangerous materials. I think we've got one around here somewhere . . .'

He turned to a pigeon-holed desk and riffled through a few stacks of paper, then shook his head. 'Or maybe not. There may be some in the back room.'

'What about the other one – 739/H-F?'

'No, we're out of those. I had to look round when Number 2 called to tell me you might be by. He said you deserved all the help I could give you, but I just don't think we have those forms.'

'Who would?'

'Stationery generally carries a full line of everything in print locally. Across the plaza, left at the bandstand and down the steps.'

'739/H-F and 8704/S. Any others?'

'Not that I can think of. Now, if you ever want to burn anything big with it, you'll want Form 2246 – that requires a couple of days' notice so the Fire Brigade can help you with the job.'

'If I ever want to burn anything large, I'll be sure the Fire Brigade is fully informed. But I only want to burn this a little at a time, in enclosed spaces. I don't suppose you have any petrol here?'

'Just a bit in the back room I use for cleaning up. If a pint or two would help, you might see the Chemist's – that's around on the far side of the Green Dome, under that big flowering tree.'

'The dogwood.'

'I suppose. Anyway, they'd have some there. It'd only be in a bottle y'know – not a tin.'

'I know. I could always use it around the workshop – for cleaning up. Do you have grease? Motor oil?'

'Oil, but no grease. And it's rather light oil.'

'Where would the Maintenance staff get grease? Those electric carts have grease nipples on the axle bearings.'

'Why, I never thought. You might ask them if they could spare some, or where they ordered it.'

'I think I will. Thank you for your help, Number 26. Be seeing you.'

*

Number 48 returned from the back of the Stationery Shop and shook her pretty head. 'I'm awfully sorry, Number 6, but we just don't seem to have any copies of Form 739/H-F at all. There's a memo in the file to the effect that they were requisitioned from the Village Hall nearly a month ago, but I guess we haven't heard anything on it. Perhaps if you went to see Number 11 up there, he could help you. Anyway, now you'll want one of these 8704/S's to go to Housing, and one to Safety, and you'll probably want a copy to keep for reference while you're preparing the storage area. Oh – and if you do go to see Number 11, you might ask about the requisition we sent in. We're out of half a dozen other things there's very little call for.'

*

Number 35 measured the golden pint into a bottle plastered with a red FLAMMABLE label. 'There you are, Number 6. We really don't have much use for motor petrol in the Village – it's a *clean* place. One of the things I've always liked about it.'

He stoppered the bottle carefully and handed it over the counter to Number 6. 'Use it sparingly – I've got less than a gallon left in stock now. I'd reorder, but I haven't been able to find the proper forms. Keep it well stopped-up, and it won't evaporate.'

*

Number 11 wasn't in, and hadn't been in all day. His personal secretary, Number 18, thought he had gone to the Printer's to ask after several jobs that hadn't been completed, and he'd had a luncheon appointment with Number 2 to which he might have gone directly.

'It's just on twelve,' Number 6 pointed out. 'May I use your telephone? It's a local call.'

'Why certainly,' she said, extending him a gracefully shaped handful of plastic.

'Number 2, please,' he said to it. And, after a moment's pause, he addressed himself identically to the answering party. '. . . I'm sure he won't mind being disturbed. Tell him it's the man with the green car. . . . Yes, that's right. Thank you.'

He shifted the phone and focused a calculating smile on Number 18. 'Inasmuch as it is lunchtime, and your boss is away, will you be held in bondage here with a cold sandwich sent in or would you have . . .'

'Good afternoon, Number 6,' said a cheerful raucous voice in his ear. *'If you're calling in regard to those troublesome forms, let me assure you that I am personally investigating the situation. Number 11 is here at the moment; he spent the morning tracking down an embarrassingly simple production problem and assures me that the forms will be available very soon. In the interim, I may be able to do something – ah – unofficially to ease your privation, at least to the extent of a gallon or two. Sorry I can't pause to chat at the moment, but you aren't the only man in the Village, after all. Be seeing you.'*

The disconnection tapped his eardrum and he looked up to see Number 18 standing with her sporty little cap in her hand. 'I take it you got your party,' she said with a twinkle as he replaced the hand set on the desk. 'In answer to your last question, I have an hour for lunch starting at twelve. And I usually eat on the Terrace when the weather is nice.'

'It's lovely today,' he said. 'I eat there myself – when I'm in town.' He smiled at her with his eyes to see if she would respond. When she did, he added, 'And over lunch I'd like to see what else we have in common.'

*

He found her a passable companion, amicable without being demanding, and a mine of information on Village politics and staff level sentiment. If he was to play their game, knowledge of the field was essential. As his self-imposed daily schedule, a trained-in habit pattern keyed by the Village environment and designed to keep him at his peak condition and as fully informed as was possible, took shape again in the following weeks, he found luncheon on the Terrace with Number 18 becoming part of it – a harmless lightly sexual spice with lunch and no more, as he discovered in her nothing to interest him personally beyond her conversational capabilities.

He rose within five minutes either way of 7:30, took a brisk run before breakfast and a long walk around the Village after, followed by a few hours work-out, a quick shower, and lunch. After lunch he would attend to business around the Village, listen to a concert by the Village Band, or sun himself on the seawall for an hour. On days when summer had the upper hand, he might go for a swim in the mid-afternoon or play a few rounds of chess on the Terrace. Leisure he had never found a problem, and with the challenge of a project like his KAR 1260 to occupy his attention, his evenings were never empty. He would usually lay down his tools and straighten the workshop when the eleven o'clock bell tolled over the Village from the tower on the hill. Then, drawing on his coat against the mists that rose from the sea and stole through the cobbled streets, he would make one last walking tour of the Village, silent and sleeping, to return to his London flat shortly after the twelve strokes of midnight and retire near 12:30.

He weekly cultivated an acquaintance with Number 40, proprietrix of the Artist's Shoppe, who incidentally supplied him with small quantities of paint thinner which he used to clean his hands and tools. This allowed him to hoard the begged pints of petrol in his workshop, where he fed them to his engine by a siphon directly to the carburettor.

On afternoons when the weather was less halcyon, he would tinker with the machine. It would not stay properly tuned, and he had not been able to establish contributing factors. When running without a load at six thousand rpm exhausted a week's fuel supply in ninety seconds, sustained testing was out of the question.

One such afternoon, shortly before three, when this routine had evolved through a full cycle of the moon and more, he was checking the sparkplugs for signs of fouling or corrosion caused by the irregular quality of the fuel, which he suspected. Outside the open end of the flower-covered car-port, sunlight began to dapple through the threatening clouds and a warm breeze sprang up.

When next he chanced to glance in that direction, it was to see a mature, apparently tame, black cat wander around the corner of the Basic Cottage Unit and stand regarding him appraisingly. He regarded it back, and after several seconds it deliberately sat down, closed its eyes, and turned its head some sixty degrees away from him. Considering, he returned to his work. As long as the animal didn't blunder into something, it was welcome to investigate. He had nothing to hide – yet – and didn't care who knew it.

He remembered noticing the cat here and there, now and then, about the Village, but he had never accorded it any particular interest; no more than it had shown in him – until now.

A minute or two later, the front door sounded its cheerful chime. He set the plugs gently on the workbench and went through the back door into his kitchenette as the chimes rang again.

At the front door was one of the little electric carts used for general transportation around the Village with its red-striped fringed awning and its straw-hatted and blazered driver. Under the awning stood eight five-gallon tins with sealed caps and diagonal red and yellow striping. In the hand of the driver, who leaned casually against the doorpost, was a plastic clipboard with several pages attached and a ball-point pen on a chain.

'Number 6?' he asked, straightening. 'If you'll sign these three copies in the box at the bottom, I've got forty gallons of hydrocarbon fuel for you. There's a data sheet stuck to one of the cans listing chemical content or something – I expect you'll know what it means.'

Forty gallons! Dazzled by his good fortune and with pictures of half-mile runs along the hard-packed beach sands at low tide in his mind, he initialled the three forms while Number 94 unloaded the heavy cans in pairs from the back of the little truck to the path.

Number 6 hoisted the first pair as the truck purred off, and bore them back through his sitting room, observing the black cat nosing about in the kitchenette as he passed through the workshop. After three more round trips his fuel was safely stored, and he returned to find the cat sitting in the middle of the carpet, fastidiously preening its shoulder.

He left it to its own interests and sat down, spark plugs postponed, to consider the largesse which had so miraculously been bestowed upon him. Forty gallons! The temptation to use it too quickly was recognised and quelled – at least half of it would go into storage somewhere until he could arrange a practical hiding place. And yet, suddenly to have forty gallons of top-quality petrol after nursing a thirsty engine on drops and counting cubic centimetres like a miser! Fine; they couldn't guess at any remotely consistent rate of consumption through that much, and he would be able to run out twice as fast without arousing a whisper of suspicion.

What he would do with it was another problem. The KAR would barely fit through the narrow cobbled streets of the Village, and there was nowhere to go in any case. Time would bring data to inspire ideas, and circumstances to take advantage of could only be recognised, seldom arranged. . . .

The black cat stood up deliberately and stalked across the carpeted floor to stand before his knees, looking up at him. He looked back, really becoming aware of the animal for the first time. Its eyes were a deep gemstone green, and they looked into his grey ones for several seconds without blinking. He shifted his weight slightly. The cat glanced down, then crouched, looked up and sprang lightly into his lap. There it rose straight-legged and formal and turned to study his face doubtfully.

He returned its scrutiny. The exact quality of the eyes, the pink maze within the ears, the texture and growth pattern of the fur, the delicate tips of nacreous claws retracted between velvet pads, all seemed realistically detailed – but he had uncertain memories of mechanical devices in the guise of living things, guided to work secretly against him. He recognised the thought, dispassionately labelled it *paranoid*, and tagged it specifically to the Village environment. Insanity can be a necessity for survival.

This seemed to be a real cat – but it had behaved in an inexplicable and unprecedented manner. By his limited acquaintance with cats it had done nothing outside the wide range of normal feline behaviour, except for its sudden interest in him. So he examined it closely for seams or subtler clues to indicate a mechanical construction. A socially acceptable animal like this would make an ideal design for a robot surveillance device – and, all things considered, that made as likely an explanation as any for why it had come into his workshop for the first time and decided to stay.

Expressionless, with just a touch of the respect due a potential bomb, he gathered it gently in his arms. It stiffened slightly at this uninvited intimacy, then relaxed; the musculature was absolutely convincing. He rubbed it behind the ears and around the side of the neck, fingers probing gently into the fragile intricacies of bone and cartilage under the warm, sliding skin as it lifted its head and started to purr. Even the purr felt right.

He shifted his weight by way of warning and felt the furry body stiffen instantly. He gathered it closer to him and stood up, holding it to his chest, and stroked its head until the tension drained out and the legs relaxed their pressure against his body. Slowly, still petting it, he rolled the cat over in his arms so that its legs were up, green eyes lidded to gleaming slits. Then, suddenly and without warning, he dropped it.

A galvanised tangle of tail and legs scrambled frantically in mid-air for a quarter of a second before the cat landed flatfooted, fur abristle and looking around for an enemy. Then abruptly it sat down and began to wash itself.

He stood looking down at it for some time, then stepped over it and went into the kitchen. In the refrigerator, a piece of fish he had brought home for dinner surrendered half an ounce to his fingers. It smelled fresh – and he closed the insulated door and took it to the front room.

The cat stood up as he entered, stretched, and wandered curiously toward the bedroom. He squatted and clucked his tongue, extending the sliver of fish to the animal. It turned and looked at the sound, then wandered back to sniff cautiously at the offering from a few inches away. It made a tiny sound like a refined snort, then turned and stalked into the bedroom.

He watched it out of sight around the door, its tail a ten-inch question mark. Then he looked back at the fish in his hand. He mashed it lightly and sniffed at it – nothing wrong. He bit off a corner and crushed it between his front teeth, studying texture and taste. Nothing sensible wrong with it.

He laid the questioned piece of fish on a paper in a corner and temporarily assigned the cat the status of Probably Real. Then he returned to his workshop, leaving the back door partly open.

An hour later, when the daylight began to fail, he went back inside to find the paper clean and the cat asleep in a corner of the sofa. It slept there while he prepared and ate dinner.

*

Two days later, about 10:30 in the morning, Number 6 jingled the bell beside a chill cabinet displaying a few moderately appetising cuts of meat, and cheerful Number 61 came out of the back, wiping bloody hands on a piece of rag, to help him.

'Lovely morning, Number 6. Fortunate you dropped in – I have some very fine veal which just arrived, and some lamb kidneys. If you'd like to take a look . . .' He pulled out a steel tray with a gesture which implied a black velvet case and a proffered loupe. The veal was white, with the slightly greenish tinge which proved proper feeding.

'So I see. Yes, very nice. It might be a bit dry, but a touch of Marsala should do it. Let me have a pound of each. And a half-pound of your less prepossessing liver – I seem to have a house guest.'

'Staying long?' Number 61 threw the veal knuckle across his block and began knocking off a pair of fine-fibred fillets.

'I have no idea. Do you recall seeing a black cat wandering about the Village? Have you any idea who owns it?'

'Nobody ever owned a cat, Number 6. I've seen him from time to time, but I've no idea where he came from or where he sleeps.'

'Nobody is responsible for feeding him?'

'No – guess he just fends for himself. It's a good thing for me people can't do that or I'd be out of business.' He weighed the meat and wrapped it, then counted kidneys on to the scale until the pointer hovered just under a pound. He dropped one more and wrapped the small pile. Then a half-pound of liver was sliced and weighed. As he worked, Number 61 offered, 'By the by, I have a bit of haddock left over from yesterday. I was about to throw it away, but he might like it. I'll make him a present of it.'

'Thanks on his behalf. Be seeing you.'

*

Shortly past two the following day, his front door chimed and a moment later Number 2 walked in. Number 6 looked up from his notes and said, 'I don't believe I heard anyone invite you in.'

'Don't be rude to your most loyal admirer, Number 6. I can allow you to be terse, but incivility, if you recall deQuincy, is the first step on the –'

'The last. "If once a man indulges himself in Murder, very soon he comes to robbing; and from robbing to drinking and from that to incivility and procrastination." It's from *Murder As A Fine Art*. I've always understood he was referring to the social preferences of the crimes.'

'It was foolish of me to venture on to such familiar

ground with you, Number 6. You were quite a professional in murder for some time, as I recall.'

The pencil did not break in his hand. After the slightest pause he said, 'And you were chiding *me* for a social crime, Number 2! Since you have brought the forbidden subject up, let me suggest you re-examine my dossier and compare it against the crimes in your own career. Or have you been a bureaucrat all your life?'

'Number 6, Number 6, now you see why I seldom call on you. I honestly walked in here with the best of intentions, and in less than a minute you have me on the defensive.' He sat down on the sofa, and the black cat lifted its head to gaze sleepily at him before returning to its nap. Number 2 noticed it with a nod.

'You seem to have found one friend in the Village, at any rate.'

'Merely a passing acquaintance,' said the unwilling host. 'It walked in a few days ago and hasn't walked out yet.'

'Have you named her?'

It was on the tip of his tongue to say the animal was not his to name, but he tapped the pencil lightly on the desk a moment, and then said, 'Oh, I was thinking of calling it Number One.'

'Really, Number 6, you must stop these witty sallies. I came here to take you for a short ride; if you continue to bait me so masterfully, the daylight will be gone and my surprise for you will fall flat. Besides, I expect you'll want to play with it yet today.' He stood and beckoned Number 6 impatiently after him.

Reluctantly, intrigued, he put down his pencil and rose from the desk. Outside an awninged electric cart waited to carry them, humming, with Number 2 at the tiller, through half a mile or more of narrow, winding, bordered lanes out of the central part of the Village and among wind-wrought native trees to a cleared patch. A rough shelter some ten by fifteen feet stood by what looked like a fairly good hard-dirt track which bent out of sight a short distance away in either direction.

Number 2 parked the cart by the shelter, and both got out. 'Well, Number 6, what do you think of it?'

'Out of context? I'd hate to spend the winter in it. Or is it a tram stop?'

'It's only meant to keep wind and rain and dust and sunlight off you and your car. If you wish a furnished *pied-à-terre* you'll have to build it yourself. But we thought you might like something simple and handy to the track.'

They now stood beside the building in question. It was about the size of the workshop behind his flat, but bare-walled and unflowered.

'You mean . . .?' He gestured with his arm.

'Yes; I've got you a place to drive. I must say it took a bit of work clearing and tamping, but you couldn't very well be expected to put as much devotion as you do into that lovely machine without any opportunity to take it out for a run.' He walked to the middle of the track and looked around. 'It's a half-mile, more or less oval and fairly flat. The hills, and the sea-cliff to the left, limited us.'

'It's a bit far from town. How do I get my car here – disassemble it and transport it piece by piece?'

'It should be possible to drive here. In bottom gear, of course, and with the greatest of care, you might be able to fit through the streets between here and there. We would have to warn pedestrians and electric carts out of the way, of course –'

'Perhaps a man could walk ahead of me waving a red flag.'

Number 2 nodded seriously. 'That is most likely what we shall have to do.'

'Speaking of electric carts – I shall need a few pounds of grease and a few quarts of oil.'

'Oil? I thought you got oil at the ironmonger's.'

'Only light and medium machine oil, which breaks down at engine temperatures. I'll probably need a requisition form for the oil, but I haven't been able to find anyone who knows.'

'What have you been using for oil?'

'My KAR had a full crankcase of nearly-new oil when it came here. I haven't had any occasion to put it to heavy use. But I shall want a change shortly if I'm actually to have a place to drive. As for the grease, I imagine you'll have some to spare close by.'

'Grease? Me?'

'You as a personification of the Village –'

'I'm honoured.'

'– maintain these electric carts, on which I observe standard grease nipples. Since axles and bearings require the same care regardless of motive power, there is a source of grease convenient to you.'

'My word! Indeed there must! I never considered the carts in terms of machinery, and all this sort of thing is left to my staff. Why, if you'd asked me about grease, I wouldn't have had the least idea beyond a Special

Requisition, and they're never heard from again. How fortunate you thought of it.'

'It was elementary.'

'But you will be able to drive for a little while, won't you?' Number 2 paced idly back and forth across the track, his face showing concern. 'I mean, you won't be delayed while we find you grease and oil. You have air for your tyres, distilled water for your battery.'

'Yes.'

'And petrol – I spent some time making a fuss on your behalf, by the way – has your petrol arrived yet? I'd been meaning to ask.'

'It arrived three days ago. Forty gallons, and top quality.'

'Well, you should have petrol to burn, then. I hope it will prove adequate for a few weeks.'

'It would go farther if I had a larger track – I shan't be able to get into top gear if this is only a quarter mile on a side, and petrol consumption skyrockets at low speeds.'

'I'd read somewhere that the most efficient operation was generally obtained at around thirty miles an hour.'

'In stock automobiles. They're designed to operate in that range. But KAR 1260 is made to my own personal tastes, and is a little less . . . conservative.'

'Really! With all your insistence on the superiority of the individual over the group, I would have thought you the archest of conservatives.'

'I thought we had agreed not to bring politics into the conversation again.' He looked around the track, then squinted at the sun. 'If you could arrange for that man you mentioned with a red flag to come by my flat, I will be ready to drive here in half an hour. And incidentally, what are the possibilities of having electricity laid on?'

*

He was at the track before 4:00 o'clock. Number 213 sat down in the shade of the shelter and propped his red flag against the wall. 'Will you be long, Number 6?'

'I may be here until dark. Would you like to go and come back with a red lantern?'

'Number 2 suggested I have one ready.' He pulled a flat battery pack from his jacket pocket. 'If you decide to leave the car here overnight and walk back, I'll be happy to keep you company on the way. And when you want to bring the car back, you can call me.'

'I won't drive back this afternoon. Why don't you just take the rest of the day off?'

Number 213 grinned up at him. 'Thanks, but I'd like to stay and watch for a little while. I've always liked cars. That's why Number 2 asked me to do this for you. They always try to give people the jobs they most enjoy. You don't mind if I just sit here for a while, do you?'

He tapped his index finger on the polished steering wheel for a second or so. He wanted to walk once around the track, checking the surface texture and layout – he didn't even know how the putative half-mile course was shaped, since most of it was hidden by trees and irregularities in the infield. But he hesitated to walk off and leave his machine alone with this grinning imbecile who burbled happily of liking cars. Perhaps his company was preferable to the uncertainty of leaving him behind.

He killed the engine and stepped out. 'I thought I'd look over the track once on foot before I tried to drive it. Want to come along?' Number 213 rose from his seat against the wall, nodding happily like an eager dog invited for a walk, and padded after him.

The track proved short indeed, being barely five hundred double paces around the centreline, but adequately surfaced. It was an eccentric oval, with the longest straight-away being about two hundred and fifty yards. The track was about fifteen feet wide, and trees had been cut back from it for another fifteen feet. The centre of the oval was a grove of tangled Mediterranean pines and cypresses like the surrounding woods, which would serve to shield this eyesore from the Village proper and absorb most of the noise he would be generating.

Then, as long as he was here and ready, and had waited so long, he started the KAR and drove a few leisurely circuits of the track, feeling out the remembered controls, listening keenly to the sound of the engine and every moving part, sensing the subtle vibrations of the suspension, reawakening the dormant reflexes which made him a part of his machine. Gradually he took the right-hand curves faster, gearing down for torque and accelerating until the approaching corner forced him to slow before throwing a skid and risking damage against the trees or wearing more rubber off the precious (and probably irreplaceable) tyres.

Eventually Number 213 lost interest in watching him go round and round and wandered away with a wave which he hardly noticed. It was nearly impossible to reach a speed greater than fifty miles per hour, and that only with the full

– and uncomfortably brief and intermittent – effort of the eight pulsing cylinders under the lean green bonnet. He couldn't maintain an average over thirty-five, and that only between twenty-five in the corners and hitting forty in the straights. He could give the engine a more even high-speed workout in the lower gears, but that became a strain on the transmission, and forging gears was still beyond his technical capability.

When he returned the car to its shelter on the Village side of the South Turn by the light of long-cold headlamps, he made a mental note to drive anti-clockwise next time, and alternate to keep the steering gear and tyre wear balanced. He was surprised to note how late it was when he returned, on foot, to his London flat to share an improvised supper with his black-furred guest.

*

In the next twelve days Number 6 grew to know and hate every tree, every bush, every stone, every leaf lining the track. At thirty-five miles per hour he passed them twenty times a day, sometimes from one side and sometimes from the other, which helped, but not much.

At last one afternoon when he came out to the track, he passed the KAR where it stood in the shelter with scarcely a glance and walked on down the track past the north end of the oval. He had surveyed that barren area beyond the last line of trees cursorily in the process of checking the track for security – he had found two wide-angled pickup cameras covering the track from convenient trees, one with a clear view into the open end of the shelter. Now it was time for a more thorough study of the ground between the North Bend of the track and the sheer cliff another half-mile away.

Beyond the trees it sloped roughly, steeper to the left than to the right. Near where the smooth wall of granite rose two hundred feet from the narrow end of the beach, the seacliff slanted down to the sand to meet it at a point where a stream must have run ten thousand years before. A furlong to the right the barren ground came level with the end of the track, and above that, sparsely, the trees began again.

Bounded by sea, stone and trees, the area in the middle was a rugged, ragged wilderness of boulders, gullies, scrub brush and bare dirt. He spent the full afternoon exploring it, nosing uphill as far as the trees to the east before the bobbing pastel spheres of Guardians came whiffling through the woods ahead of him. He stood his ground and spoke to them gently; since his track had been kept so free of them, he expected no interference here. They paused at the edge of the trees and flobbed menacingly, but made no further advance.

Willing not to press the confrontation, Number 6 withdrew and carried his survey downhill to the sea. When he had finished, he returned home and spent the evening sketching things in a large notebook.

*

As the tower bell rang the hour of 4:00, he came up the steps to the Green Dome. Doors opened silently before him until he stood before the tall white double panels with a tasteful '2' in bronze at eye-level. He paused, knowing his arrival had not been unobserved, and waited until these too swung inward.

Number 2 looked up from a flickering panel set in his desk with an acceptable imitation of surprise. 'Why, Number 6! I was just wondering about you. Can you stay for tea? You seem to be in quite a hurry.'

'I may grant you the pleasure of my company – I thought you might know where I could pick up another set of petrol requisitions and help me push them through.'

'More petrol? Already? When Number 213 mentioned you spent all day going around and around that track, I must admit I was gratified. But I seem to recall you said it would last you a month.'

'I would never had made so specific an estimate. I have less than five gallons left, and that won't last another week. And while we're on the subject, I haven't heard anything about the motor oil either. I'll need at least ten litres, thirty-weight, non-detergent.'

'I shall see to it. Did you get the grease from Maintenance? Oh, please don't stand –' He pressed a button to produce a chair into which Number 6 sank and crossed his legs.

'Yes – a couple of pounds. Quite satisfactory. Number 99 was good enough to bring a gun and give me a free mechanical inspection. She was quite impressed.'

'I should imagine. Tea?'

'Thank you.'

Number 2 generated a beautiful porcelain cup made of insulating plastic and filled with steaming Earl Grey as Number 6 continued.

'Now about the length of the track – I appreciate the fact

that I have a place to drive at all, but it's simply not big enough. There is open space to the north to extend it; how do I go about getting this done?'

'But that is park land, Number 6. It's supposed to be for the use of the whole Village. You already have three or four acres all of your very own.'

'You can't play soccer on a chess board. I have seen no one else making use of that part of the grounds. Most of my present four acres is still available for picnics – the infield is maintained as a wilderness area. All I need is room to extend the track, down that barren slope into the rill.'

'Well, I really don't know, Number 6. The subject could be brought up at the Village Council, but I expect they would feel that enough of our limited land has already been placed at your personal disposal.'

'I doubt they would notice if the track was extended. The natural contour conceals it from the Village and would deflect the sound as well as the trees block it now. How the good Villagers would react to it, as you very well know, depends on how it is presented to them. What if they were to discover, without any fanfare, that the track was there and in use, causing no particular inconvenience to anyone?'

'Your attitude is shocking, Number 6 – shocking! I could have no part in such an . . . such an *unmutual* deception.'

'You needn't. Tea?'

'Thank you. I must warn you against assuming responsibilities you have no right to.'

'A man has the right to any responsibility he can handle. Whereas you feel that the fewer responsibilities a man has, the better.'

'It's certainly easier to consolidate them in trustworthy

hands. Leaves so much more time and effort free for other things. More efficient, more practical. Why should everyone make their own shoes? Hunt their own food? Till their own fields? You delegate responsibility for your health to a doctor, for your welfare to a lawyer, for your nourishment to total strangers – I don't believe I've seen you smile before, Number 6.'

'I find little to amuse me here.'

'Your own personal nourishment, I am aware, is a matter of considerable concern on your part; I was speaking in a much larger sense. But you take advantage of professionally prepared food – when it is a matter of convenience. Even you have heated cans of soup during your wide experience. The median man survives largely by the efforts of others while he pursues his own individual goals as best he can. Why, I don't even know the Number of my own cook.'

'*The median man*. The expression interests me – the statistical excuse for your actions?'

'That's an oversimplification.'

'But an accurate one.'

Number 2 shrugged. 'Relative accuracy,' he said, dismissing the subject with his tone of voice. 'The median man is the statistical individual for whom the greatest amount of effort produces maximal results. The social equivalent of the physical measurements used in designing automobiles, theatre seats and beds. For that matter, as the distance between bookshelves is designed to fit the "median book."'

'A non-professional acquaintance of mine claimed to have been connected with the St. Lawrence Seaway construction project, and he swore that the engineering facility in charge of bridging operations took careful measurements of all vessels capable of negotiating the Seaway and built all the bridges with five feet of clearance for the average funnel height. I never believed him, myself.'

'Number 6, your parables astound me. Have we been knocking your funnels off? I myself have been – in several senses – moving heaven and earth to build a series of by-pass canals, drawbridges, locks and tunnels so you can drive your car, fuel your car and tinker with your car to your heart's content!'

'Out of the boundless charity you feel towards all living creatures.'

'My job here is to make you happy – but it includes seeing that you don't bother other people any more than is absolutely necessary. This was a happy Village until you came here, Number 6, and I must say frankly that I look upon you as a challenge in this matter. Is dissatisfaction so deeply bred into your personality that you can never be happy anywhere?'

'Make me happy. Get me that motor oil and fifty gallons of the same mixture as before. Your man can come around for the seven empty cans at his leisure.'

'You are so single-minded, Number 6. Of course I shall do all I can to expedite your petrol requisition, though it may take a fortnight. The oil should come with it. I do appreciate your bridge parable, honestly; what you mean is that we don't allow enough for exceptions. We really do all we can, but our motto has never been able to reach beyond *The Greatest Good For The Greatest Number*

'Any quantity of individuals can be effectively handled in

statistical form – the same formulae can tell how many people are watching a given television broadcast or how many will die in a given holiday weekend. These mathematical models are of demonstrable accuracy and are identical to those which predict natural radioactive decay in a mass of unstable atoms. The behaviour of individuals is of no statistical consequence – whether five hundred people or five hundred and one are killed by motor accidents in Bank Holiday traffic matters not the slightest except to the personal acquaintances and intimates of the five-hundred-and-first; the social impact, the public outcry for safer streets would not be substantially altered by one death, or a dozen. A hundred more or less would barely gain recognition as a significant factor.'

'Unless the five-hundred-and-first is a politician or a film star.'

'That only enlarges the effective circle of acquaintances. There again you have tried to make an exception destroy a generality. Exceptions are to generalities what holes are to a sponge. A few more or less don't matter – statistically.'

'But if the sponge had no holes at all, it wouldn't hold water.'

'And if pigs had wings they'd be pigeons! Honestly, Number 6, I had promised myself I would not be drawn into argument with you again. Do go away and let me get back to my work – you'll have your petrol.'

'Thank you, Number 2. Be seeing you.'

*

For the next two days Number 6 walked around the barren

area north of the track, pacing off distances, sighting past large rocks, trees and major irregularities in the ground, poking at the earth here and there like a prospective builder looking over a site.

The black cat followed him there the first day, wandering along behind him, beside him, in front of him, stopping at will or disappearing to reappear later, as if bound entirely on business of its own, and while he surveyed, the cat prowled around the rugged field, hunting its own game.

That same afternoon he had the opportunity to observe an educational confrontation, and was pleased with what he learned: fortune placed him at the side of a thickly gnarled bush twice his height when a moving white shape caught his eye and he froze against the bush to watch a Guardian bounding lugubriously toward him.

As he watched, it swerved toward a darting black shape in the scrubby grass and picked up speed. The cat sped across an open space, tail a-bristle; the spheroid took to the air in fourteen-foot leaps, quivering like a berserk custard ball. The cat doubled on its tracks and shot through the shadow of the Guardian in mid-leap, dodging out of sight down a gully in a few seconds.

Number 6 ducked back around the bush as the sphere fought its momentum to turn and follow its quarry; by the time it rolled vaguely off in the direction the cat had taken the trail was cold. The uncanny thing hesitated, searched blindly for a minute or so, then trundled off absentmindedly in the general direction of the Village.

When it was gone, Number 6 came out. He had probably had no real reason to hide from the thing – it wasn't one of the dangerous ones, and he had every right to be here. Well, nearly every right.

The cat was sitting beside the back door washing itself when Number 6 returned to his flat a few hours later, and seemed satisfied with the chicken giblets supplied by the good butcher that morning (as they were two days old).

*

After another day of study he had determined the optimum layout for the projected extension of his track. The following morning he set out on his regular tour of the Village, and encountered, after two-thirds of a casually meticulous search of the town, three men in overalls riding in an electric cart. He hailed them.

'Where are you going?'

'Reseeding the South Walk.'

'Ah, then you're the ones I was looking for. The reseeding job can wait – you're to come with me. Number 55, can you fetch that small bulldozer I saw shoving around debris on the beach after the storm last month?'

'Uh, certainly, Number – uh . . .'

'Good. Does it have a roller or a grader attachment of some sort?'

'Well, it's got the scraper blade. There's a power roller, but it's working out on Seaview Point all day.'

'Reserve it for next week.' He climbed into the fourth seat of the cart, next to Number 92. 'We'll go back to pick up the 'dozer with the scraper blade. Are you checked out on it?'

'Yeah –'

'Fine. Then you'll follow us to the job site. You'll be working with me.'

It was 10:00 o'clock when they stopped at the top of the uneven slope, and Number 6 spent the next forty-five minutes establishing the nature of the job to be done. He indicated the placement, direction and width of the lane he wanted scraped in the wild terrain, then joined with Numbers 84 and 92 in cutting down one tree and rooting out a number of rocks before lunch. They met again at 2:00 and worked until dusk.

At half past nine that evening. Number 2 greeted him from his television which he had unplugged. 'Number 6, what is this I hear about you kidnapping three workmen this morning?'

'I used no particular coercion; I caused no particular trouble.'

'How long did you plan to keep them from their proper jobs? That reseeding was part of our entire spring schedule – if part of the Village fails to bloom this summer, yours will be the blame.'

'I'll give you back Number 84, but I'd like to keep Number 92 and the bulldozer for a week. Then you can have him back too, and I'll trade the bulldozer for the heavy roller. But I want to keep Number 55.'

'Number 6, this is intolerable! This is uncountenanceable! This is impossible! This is insane! These men have their own responsibilities, their own jobs to do. I cannot possibly agree to so monstrous a bargain!'

'Thank you. I'll tell Number 84 not to mention it to anyone when he goes back reseeding tomorrow. He'll remember. He's not too bright, but he's honest and trustworthy.'

'I've always felt it a pity that those qualities correlated so closely.'

'Oh? I've generally found it the other way round. An intelligent man knows that trust is worth having.'

'Yes, and more likely to find some opportune time to betray it.'

'And less likely to betray it at some inopportune time, or by an error of judgment. An intelligent man, a man who reacts rationally, is easier to predict than a man who reacts randomly.'

'And here we return to our basic difference of opinion, Number 6. A large group of individuals reacting randomly is the easiest thing in the world to predict. Fortunately, the overwhelming majority does react randomly – the human race is a natural phenomenon. A statistical population of intelligent, self-determining individuals would be almost impossible to handle on any but the most basic, physical grounds.'

'Has it occurred to you that they might not need – or want – to be "handled"?'

'Don't bandy semantics with me, Number 6 – they will want to be fed, and clothed, and transported, and entertained and sheltered. If that particular term offends you, let us say *"served"*, even though the euphemistic loading that word has acquired offends me.'

'Why must they be served statistically rather than individually?'

'You have no concept of numbers over a few hundred! It would be humanly impossible to serve a million people individually – it is impossible to serve a thousand with any efficiency. Your petrol is an individual service, and represents a great deal more effort on our part than you seem to appreciate.'

'I *do* appreciate it, Number 2. I feel indebted to you for all you have done to make my stay here a busy one. And I will send your gardener back to his beds the first thing in the morning.'

'Thank you, Number 6. Be seeing you.'

'Be seeing you.'

*

Now Number 6 abandoned his self-imposed schedule to fill his days with physical labour and his nights with retuning the car's engine. It took a week to scrape a strip of roughly cleared earth between ten and fifteen feet wide and somewhat over a mile long. He directed the bulldozer over the course he had paced out, levelling minor irregularities in the ground to a point where his KAR could take them without undue strain on the suspension.

Then the roller was brought by a long and indirect service road maintained around the Village for that purpose, and the rubble left by the bulldozer was packed down into a passable firm surface. Number 92 was released as soon as the heavy work was done, and Number 6 worked on with the roller and Number 55 for some days more, carving a passable road out of the wilderness. They spoke seldom, sharing little but the interest in doing a job well.

Number 92 came back to help on his days off, and even the weather remained amiable. Through the whole period of work as well, they were never bothered by Guardians. Number 6 took this to mean tacit approval, and proceeded with an untroubled conscience.

At last, one afternoon, they stopped work and studied the last square yards of solidly packed earth. Number 6 nodded. 'That's good,' he said, and looked at Number 55 seated on the quietly humming tractor. 'How would you like a ride all the way around?' he asked.

Number 55 shifted to the right. 'I'll carry you back up to the shed.'

The north end of the irregular oval had touched the edge of the last row of pines – now, kinked in like a hairpin to a figure eight, the track extended another half mile down the hill and back, veering here and there to take the contours and avoid major obstacles, but with the landward leg so angled as to allow of just over a half-mile straightaway, running downhill to the north and including a straight side of the original track.

The curve at the bottom was banked and turned inland uphill for seventy yards to the rising wall of rock that stood as stark cyclorama to the whole Village, then made a sharp 180-degree to the left for a long downhill all the way to the edge of the beach, straight and smooth for a hundred and twenty yards, gently sloping to level at the bottom. At the fringe of sand, it turned left again, angled around an ancient, wave-hurled boulder half again his own height, made a long curve around two trees, cut right directly up a 25% gradiant through a cut which had cost them two days of sweat and aching muscles though it was only sixty feet long, then left up a tyre-wearing gradiant with half-a-dozen irregular switchbacks evading trees and bushes all the way to the top, where it dodged slightly left and became the landward half of the original oval, around the south end of the track back to the shelter. It would give him enough of a workout and enough opportunity to open halfway in top gear; parts of it might need a little more spade work, but he had always intended to put the final touches on the course himself. All in all, as he said to Numbers 55 and 92 over a small private celebration that evening, it was a job to be proud of – though he had in mind certain aspects of which his guests and co-workers were hopefully unaware.

*

Two weeks of physical labour had not distracted him from his KAR 1260; though he had driven less than a thousand miles his oil needed changing and he had less than a gallon of fuel left outside his inviolable cache. He took it around the track half a dozen times before reluctantly creeping back to his garage with faithful Number 213 waving the red flag before him, grimly hoping to be spared the embarrassment of running stone dry in the streets and having to be pushed home.

He had about fifteen gallons cached from the forty he'd received nearly a month ago – five gallons less than he'd hoped to save, but his fuel consumption figures simply could not be padded by more than 60% and remain remotely acceptable to Number 2. Besides, the volatile fluid had proved a problem to store securely; something would have to done about that before he could put away much more.

*

The motor oil arrived four days after his track was finished – the full ten quarts he had requested. But he had to return to the Chemist's Shop for two pints of petrol to warm his engine again when he changed the oil.

Number 2 assured him regularly that his petrol should arrive any day. On the days when it didn't, Number 6 contented himself with walking around the enlarged track once every afternoon in addition to his other regular peripatetic exercises. In the evening he would polish the chromework or buff another coat of wax into the instrument panel. When this palled, he busied himself with pencil and paper, roughing out notes and sketches of sleekly streamlined shapes, doodling airflow lines around them, estimating cross-sections, plugging arbitrary values into arcane formulae while the black cat dozed on the hearthrug before the unlit electric fire.

The arrival of thirty gallons of fuel was as unheralded as the previous delivery; his doorbell chimed one evening at half-past seven and Number 94 straightened from an identical slouch against his doorpost to extend a clipboard with the forms. This time there were only six of the red-and-yellow tins, and Line 8 had '30' instead of '40' written on it – it would be worse than useless to question the messenger, since if something was wrong with the order, it obviously shouldn't be delivered. Again he initialled the forms in the space left for his Number – they'd accepted it last time without a murmur.

But did this mean they were going to reduce his supply? Had they kept closer track of his fuel consumption that he'd allowed for? It took him ten minutes to get the six cans stowed neatly beneath the workbench, and as he worked he calculated odds. All factors considered, he saw no reason to abandon his primary plan – which called for him to do nothing unusual for another fortnight. He would have to drive with caution and economy at all times, since his primary plan included at least fifty gallons of petrol.

His face registered none of the grim purpose in his mind, and when he returned to the sitting room he cleared his conscious mind of all secret thoughts and dwelt upon the delight of having petrol to burn again. He telephoned Number 213 to request his services at nine o'clock next morning, then poured himself a glass of dry sherry, inspected his small collection of records which had been duplicated or transported with him, and settled back to surround himself with the crystalline structures of electronically synthesised Bach.

Some time later he became aware of a light warmth against his hand, and looked down to find the cat curled up beside him. When he returned from turning the record over, the animal lifted its black head to be petted as he sat down beside it. He refilled his glass and leaned back in his chair. As the patterns of the music interwove about him, he felt a gradual easing of the tensions within him – almost for the first time in the Village he was beginning to feel at ease.

The cat purred soundlessly under his caressing fingers, and as his eyes closed it suddenly occurred to him that he could say, considering, that at this point Number 2's expressed desire had been fulfilled; he was happy. but since the core of this joy was the relentless progression of his own secret goals as opposed to – or even parallel to – those goals proposed by Number 2, he felt fully justified in seeming satisfied with the present situation. In fact, it was important to his covert expectations that he must continue to appear at least as satisfied and cooperative as he did. He did not resent the fact that assuming the appearance was presently far from difficult.

He maintained it well for the week he had determined on, and then he went to see Number 2 again early one afternoon.

'You're early for tea, Number 6. Don't you ever think of ringing up before you call?'

'I see no reason to duplicate effort – you know where I am every minute anyway.'

'Do you think this entire Village is run for your benefit alone? And even if it were, do you think I am so desperate for diversion that I would spend every waking moment studying you like a jealous lover?'

'Like an entomologist, perhaps. I expect you, personally, have other things to do than watch over me day and night, but then I seldom consider you, personally. You are the personification of the Village. You probably deserve the Royal Plural in your address, as such. A pity Modern English lacks a specific second plural.'

'You flatter me. Don't tell me you need more fuel already?'

'I shall shortly. Have you inspected the recent extension of –'

'I don't want to hear about it. Number 6, I was humiliated – *humiliated!* – in counsel session when Number 4 brought up the matter of a hundred and nine unauthorised man-hours expended on that . . . that *project* of yours! Not to mention machine-hours and energy expended, schedules thrown off for weeks in half a dozen departments . . . You certainly created a pretty mess.'

'I trust no permanent damage was done.'

'No – the Village will bloom more or less as scheduled, though perhaps not quite as fully flowered as it might have been. I only hope you're satisfied now.'

'It will hold me for a while. But now that I have farther to drive, I'll need more petrol. There is no point in continuing these monthly dumb-shows – I will continue to need fifty gallons a month to drive as I wish.'

'That is utterly out of the question, Number 6! With a degree of regularity, we might be able to arrange for twenty or even twenty-five gallons on a monthly basis, depending on your actual consumption, of course.'

'Two litres of oil monthly.'

'One'

'Impossible.'

'You should be able to drive two thousand miles on a change of oil. At fifteen miles to the gallon, that would take one hundred and thirty-five gallons of petrol, perhaps one hundred and fifty. At twenty-five gallons a month, that's one oil change every six months . . .'

'At ten litres per change, allowing another litre every three months for loss and margin, that comes to two litres a month.'

'So it does. Very well, in addition to the regular litre each month, we can arrange for six litres when you want a change.'

'Very well. But my fuel consumption has been closer to

ten or twelve miles to the gallon. Keep that in mind when you're calculating my ration.'

'Ten or twelve? I should have thought you would be squeezing twenty miles per gallon, with all the care you seem to take.'

'Performance can always use improvement. I hadn't even hoped to get better than fifteen, and I think, considering the displacement, I've done fairly well.'

'Mechanical devices are not my forte, Number 6. I shall be delighted to help you whenever possible, but don't attempt to communicate with me on a technical level. I'm more of theoretician, I'm afraid.'

'Most people who want to run other people's lives for them are theoreticians.'

'Is your chief hobby automobiles or debating? I shan't invite you to stay for tea today – I have several important people coming on business which, as you may or may not believe, actually has nothing at all to do with you.'

'I intend to remind you daily until my petrol arrives.'

'Then I will not be in. Good afternoon, Number 6 – you have all the promises you are going to get from me this time.'

'Then good afternoon. Be seeing you.'

*

Miraculously, twenty gallons of petrol arrived within a week. His driving schedule increased to the putative limits of his fuel supply, and after another fortnight he called one morning on Number 40 at the Artist's Shoppe just off the Village green. She displayed an introductory kit for leather-working, and he asked about the materials and techniques of moulding and sculpting in fibreglass.

He found sheets of glass fibre were formed and impregnated with an epoxy cement which supplied the toughness and resilience which the glass alone would lack, while the glass itself lent the essential structural strength. As Number 40 described casting various small objects, then lining the moulds with glass cloth, she located a colourfully lithographed box which contained a Fibreglass Starter Kit.

'Here we are, Number 6. This includes complete instructions for two projects which will familiarise you with the techniques. If you've never worked with it before, you may find it a bit sticky at first.'

'Perhaps I'd better take that. But I had something larger in mind – too large to mould, actually. Can I form this over a framework?'

'I should think so . . . Just how large were you thinking of?'

'I should like to cover about seventy-five square feet with a three-eighths-inch thickness – or a centimetre.'

'Seventy-five square *feet*? What are you planning on building – an addition to your cottage?'

'As a matter of fact, I was thinking of designing a racing fairing of some kind for my automobile. Perhaps I might even try replacing the entire coachwork with a fibreglass body of my own design and construction.'

'That's an ambitious project. I hope we can help you – I don't think we've ever had a call for that much all at once. I'm not even sure the same techniques would apply to something that had to be . . . well, really *practical*. I mean, I thought you wanted to use it for a work of art!'

'Can't art be useful?'

'Oh, of course, I mean, it's nice if useful things can be artistically designed, but they have to be made – more sturdy, don't they, and there's bound to be a certain sacrifice to practicality. I was really thinking more of "Art For Art's Sake." Or something. But you might be able to find out about what you want in the Village library – there are lots of books on handicrafts and things. And there's a bibliography in the pamphlet that comes with the Fibre-glass Starter Kit.'

'You don't have any idea how long it would take to get the larger sheets.'

'I don't even know how much they'd weigh, or how they would be shipped. I'm not even sure they could be brought here. I'll see about ordering them as soon as you know how much you want and what kind. But you had best be prepared to follow up the orders yourself.'

*

A discreet tapping at the open end of his ersatz garage brought his head up from under the bonnet to find Number 2 leaning against the corner, lit by the lowering golden sunlight from the west.

'I thought I would take the opportunity to drop in on you unannounced, Number 6. Your car looks lovely.'

'Thank you. Having disposed of the social niceties, would you care for a tour of inspection? I have nothing to hide.'

'I should love to look around at another time – but there

is one point of curiosity which I should like to get out of the way first. I hear you've found a new hobby.'

'Word seems to get around.'

'In my position, I pick up most of the rumours.'

'They're remarkably vague rumours. I didn't expect to have to bother you with it, knowing how busy you are – just a sort of decorating project.'

'You must be decorating something very large. Since one of my responsibilities is the aesthetic unity of the Village, I'd like to know where you intend to display seventy-five square feet of fibreglass.'

'It will be a good deal smaller when I finish with it – I intend to design a racing fairing for my KAR. I feel that the operating efficiency I've been able to achieve could be increased materially if not significantly by the addition of a lightweight, streamlined shell. In fact, I've been considering replacing the heavy coachwork entirely.' He leaned back against the bumper and crossed his ankles.

'It'll keep the KAR out of operation for a couple of weeks,' he continued cheerfully, 'but I never have enough petrol anyway. I can save up a little while I'm working on this new project.'

'Number 6, it honestly does my heart good to see you taking so much interest in things. Idle hands are the devil's playground. I'm sure we can find you what you want. After all, our goal here is to keep you happy, and any reasonable service towards that end is our duty.'

'Your solicitude touches me deeply, Number 2.'

'But it is difficult to keep up with you much of the time. Why couldn't you have had a passion for crewel work, or badminton, or the bagpipes?'

'I might have taken up parachuting, or speedboat racing. Or amateur radio. My tastes are not especially exotic – I consider myself an easy man to please.'

'Not noticeably. But I pride myself that within our limited facilities you are kept reasonably satisfied. You shall have your fibreglass in a few weeks – until then I suggest you concentrate on refining those rough designs you have sketched out. Be seeing you.'

He straightened from the doorpost and was gone. Number 6 looked after him in the gathering twilight, and was bold enough to permit himself a smile.

Section III: Andante Captibile

'You're going to let him have the fibreglass?'

'I see no reason not to. After all, we're watching him every minute he's at work. Anything he does will be noted and anything he makes ready will be prepared for.'

'Don't you think he *knows* we're watching? Don't you think he has made allowances for that as he has every time in the past?'

'*Not* every time, Number 4 – far from it. Only once has he actually committed a totally unsupervised escape.'

'We've been lucky. Several times we haven't found out until –'

'Nonsense! Luck is a loser's excuse. We are simply on top of him every minute. Nothing he does escapes us.'

'He moves fast. And you can't follow his mind.'

'So you expect him to leave us, "sweating and swearing, a mile and a half behind"? If his mind wants to escape by itself, let it. There's five million words of escape fiction in the Village library. He can lose himself from Erech to Barsoom to Coventry. *Die Gedanken sind frei.* But if he makes the least attempt to take his body with him, we can stop it. When he learns to teleport himself, we will be defeated. I am willing to wait.'

'Mmmm. Number 2, how far from the north end of the track is our nearest Rescue Unit stationed?'

'About a mile and a half. But an amphibious Guardian is posted in the rocks at the north end of the beach less than fifty metres from the spot where the track touches the sand, and two heavy-duties are permanently stationed among the trees at the top of the rill. I don't see any way he could make it up the lowest part of the rock face in less than ten minutes, and we can gas him into a net before he's halfway to the top.'

'He's beaten the Guardians before – at least, he believes he has, which is how his behaviour will be predicted.'

'Well, what he doesn't know, in this case, will be very careful not to hurt him.'

'I still say you should never have given him tools. Any tool magnifies his ability to do things. And One knows we've nearly had problems with that in this subject before. He does enough bare-handed . . .'

'Number 4, what he *does* is all we *can* monitor. The less he does, the more I would worry. The more he does, the happier I am. For over a year, in the Village, he brooded upon his fancied "captivity" and built up a head of emotional steam which drove him to continue his attempts to escape.'

'You see, he has never had any reason to *want* to stay

here. The Village is a beautiful place. It is – beautilitarian. It is restful, peaceful and tranquil. It is Shangri-La by the seashore. But a certain personality type, with nothing to do, nothing to occupy his mind and hands, will go to amazing lengths to find a direction for his energies. What I have done is channel this *drive* into paths which are readily observable. Otherwise, how could we possibly tell what he might do if left entirely to his own devices?'

'All I'm saying is that he has too many devices. He should not have been given tools. And that engine, in the most basic terms, is a source of energy. With tools and energy people like him have been conquering the universe. Who do you think we are?'

'Do you expect him to beat his mudguards into rotor blades and depart from our midst in a fibreglass helicopter? Really, Number 4 . . .'

'I don't expect anything – or more precisely, I *do* expect anything. Don't underestimate him, Number 2. And don't overestimate yourself. He has only one thought in his mind, day and night – escape.'

'That may have been true a few months ago. But now there are, at least occasionally, moments when he thinks about his car – '

'Only in terms of escape.'

'– and the cat is definitely, observably becoming a part of his life. I shouldn't doubt he has considered taking the cat with him when he makes his next escape attempt.'

'Then you admit . . .'

'. . . Only that *currently* – or recently – he is thinking about escaping. These thoughts will gradually, imperceptibly, fade over the period of another six months through procrastination to oblivion. I felt from the very beginning that if we could just keep him here and happy for a little while, his life would come to centre around the Village. His life outside was not an especially happy one.'

'He hasn't done much towards making friends.'

'Compared to his previous record, he has been remarkably sociable. He is on nodding acquaintance with Number 40 of the Artist's Shoppe, the Chemist, the Ironmonger, the Butcher . . .'

'. . . The Baker and the Candlestick Maker. And those workmen who helped him build the track. All right, he's on a comfortable social footing in the Village. He's done that before.'

'He has never allowed anything of ours to become part of his life before.'

'The cat? All right, I'm willing to admit you did a good job on the cat. Wasn't that your conditioning apparatus?'

'Yes. Its effects are more predictable on less advanced mechanisms. We gave the animal fifteen minutes of moderate pleasure stimulation combined with Number 6's personal effluvium and voice.. We could easily have driven it to react to him as to catnip, but Number 6 is far too perceptive to let pass something as unlikely as a strange cat which suddenly demonstrates a passionate attraction for him. Even with the gentle predilection we programmed, he was unduly suspicious for some time. Fortunately, his ego permits him to think the animal could desire to stay with him. His remarkably perceptive examination of the animal was only physical – like us, he can observe only what happens. The mind is still a locked box, Number 4, and opening it from the outside tends to affect the contents, even under laboratory conditions.'

'Precisely why I object to your giving him tools. How do you know what he's thinking about doing with them?'

'Because I can – and do – influence what he thinks about. Until recently there has been nothing in the Village that *mattered* to him. He will not make friends among the Villagers – he is capable of conscious effort to avoid it, in fact – but his atrophied social instincts are at least being stimulated by the presence of the cat. Besides, at least subconsciously, he may tend to feel it's "good luck."'

'*Good luck?* Number 6?'

'I never implied he thinks of the cat as a lucky charm. But if you recall, we brought them together shortly before the delivery of his first large shipment of petrol. The learning mechanism of the brain is designed to link, at least tentatively, any unusual incidents in close temporal proximity. *That* particular mechanism is far older than the human race.'

'But he would never begin to believe . . .'

'I sincerely hope he doesn't. If he ever becomes consciously aware of it, he'll discard it automatically simply because it happened in the Village. I restimulated the pattern by giving him his short track just after he'd brought something delicate home from the butcher's for the cat. He seems more willing to let it live in his home than he was at first. And after all, this man is possessed of a fantastic psychological resistance. I shall probably reinforce the cat by letting it stay away for several days when Number 6 must suffer some setback or another, and then returning it when we do him a favour. These things take time, Number 4 –

time. You would hardly expect him to rush out and join a Fraternal Organisation.'

'Unless it was important to some goal of his own.'

'That goes without saying. But you will admit that he is becoming more a part of the Village.'

'He has only worn his Number once – that time he wore it upside down and passed as Number 9 for hours until a clerk noticed that the Ordinary behind the digit was standing on its handlebars.'

'Ah well, Number 6 has a nearly infinite capacity for painful whimsy. Still, though he is slow to adopt our ways, he is participating willingly in them more and more. He fills out our forms and follows our official procedures – anyone, no matter how stubborn, will run a maze if they see the right reward at the end. He is willing to play our game, by our rules, on our time, in order to get his precious petrol.'

'He didn't go through your channels to build that extension to his track.'

'There were no available channels for that; I expected him to do something typically audacious, and he did. It was lovely. He used every erg and calorie of energy – physical, mental, and especially emotional – in carving that highway out of the wilderness. Now it represents a personal investment in the Village. He *made* it, and he is the only person to have driven on it. In his peculiar but predictable mental set, that establishes it as his "territory," and it is a precious thing to him because of this.'

'An area of ground? How primitive!'

'Not as an area *per se* – an emotional quality surrounding this area which links it with him. Related to anthropomorphic Nature Religions in various cultures.

Bear in mind that in order to predict his reactions you must recognise the causes behind his action patterns. The reconstruction of his flat, for instance. He feels comfortable there, even though he knows consciously he is in the Village, because it is "his own." His personality is written all over it, and was perfectly simple to forge. It is as soothing to him as a roomful of mirrors to a narcissist. Consider how much of his life has been spent keeping his own company. You've studied his dossier – you know he's never been prone to form warm, normal human relationships. He hasn't had a pet since childhood.'

'Your cat took to him, Number 2, but I don't think you can say he's accorded it the status of a *pet*. He contributes just less than half the animal's nourishment – it sleeps under his roof about two-thirds of the time – it seems to prefer his company, and he doesn't object to it, but I don't think you could honestly call it a pet.'

'A free companion, then. But he shares his territory. And he is occasionally even affectionate towards the cat.'

'I can't imagine that adjective ever being applied to Number 6.'

'I have a videotape of it. Would you like to see it?'

'I'm not sure. What does it consist of?'

'Not a great deal, actually. Here, I can punch it up for you in a moment. There it is.'

. . .

'I shouldn't say "affectionate", Number 2. The cat curled up against him in the chair, and put its head under his free hand – stroking it would be an instinctive reaction. Even scratching it around the neck and behind the ears.'

'Of course it's instinctive, you ninny! We cannot

approach this man on a conscious level – how often must I explain this to you? It's instinctive, indeed – but it's an instinct he has not used before. It is the most stabilising, enervating, tranquilising instinct known. He has buried it under the calluses of years of bitter experiences. Awakened now at our will, it will put him completely within our parameters in – oh, conservatively, another year. And without any damage to the essential BGR patterning.'

'If it's awakened. Look at him. That manual action is as idle and void of emotion as drumming his fingers on a table top.'

'No. Look. The cat is purring. There's a frame coming up I want to hold for you – just when he glances down at . . . There it is. Perfectly clear. He is smiling. And it's not that damned canary-swallowing smirk he affects around me – it is an honest, sincere smile of content and pleasure. Pleasure is his *companion*, Number 4. The cat may eat and sleep where it pleases. Our concern is with Number 6, and his peace of mind. The fact that he *can* and has, even if only once, even if only for a moment, smiled like that, proves my entire case. He has been happy here for one second; therefore he can be made happy. If he can be made happy, he can be *kept* happy.'

'You cannot have the argument both ways, Number 2. If the prisoner is happy, why lock him in? If he is not, why pretend that he is?'

'Bernard Shaw was writing of marriage, Number 4, and I hardly think the quotation is apt. Our relationship is on nothing remotely approaching an equal footing – it is far more than of the parent to the child, educating and guiding, even though it may be against the momentary will of the child, for his and society's greater good. He will thank us for it, eventually.'

His inexpensive but practical ten-scale slide rule was in the left-hand waist-level drawer of the Gregorian highboy beside his broad worktable. It had told him how much fibreglass would be needed to surround KAR 1260 in an aerodynamically contoured housing, but it wasn't able to tell him what the contours should be.

Pages and pages of notes and sketches, any and all of which could bear suspicious examination, detailed the framework and bracing and mounts to the chassis of the KAR. Other, rougher, sketches had been doodled in smooth dirt with the end of a stick as a temporary aid to visualisation of certain problems in mechanical linkages which could have had nothing to do with a streamlined hull, and had been erased with a smooth shoe-sole as soon as the problem involved had been worked out. The finished drafts of these he carried in his head.

He didn't really expect the fibreglass – it would be too simple. But they'd been expecting him to ask for things, even encouraging him by being so improbably obliging. His most overt actions so far had been met with no more than mild reproof. They were obviously building him up for something. Fine. Since he couldn't guess what they were trying to do, worry about it was pointless. Instead, he would keep them busy guessing what *he* was doing.

They couldn't have bought that story about a racing fairing – Number 2 was not a complete idiot – but they had swallowed it whole with a perfectly straight face. Since he hadn't had any better ideas, he would continue until something better turned up. He was willing to play their game as long as he won his own points; if it meant playing Stirling Moss for their television cameras he was far from loath to drive around a few hours a day and cache a third of the fuel they gave towards his unexpressed needs.

They had helped him in so many ways already – could they now be coaxed just a little farther? As nearly as he had been able to fathom Number 2's character, it might even be possible. As long as he gave every evidence of being *nearly* satisfied, he might, like the cold camel in the fable, eventually take everything he wanted.

As long as Number 2 insisted on attempting to make him happy within limits, the least he could do was offer his benefactor every opportunity to pass those limits in a series of short, easy steps from one little favour to another – increments which could conceivably end with Number 2 offering him a ticket to freedom, open return – if not literally, at least practically.

In fact, the fibreglass was such a ticket – it had been reserved, even if not confirmed. With nearly thirty gallons of fuel and some oil put away he already had a feeling of accomplishment; what he needed now was something to put it in. Only some work on the transmission and assorted unlikely mechanical connections remained to be accomplished in his shop, though several of his sub-assemblies might suffer from the inability to fit certain parts together in plain sight, and several mounting holes which would need to be vertically symmetrical to within a fraction of a millimetre could never be tested before the omnipresent cameras without betraying his intentions. Only surreptitious and momentary comparisons would be possible until the actual moment of necessity – after which time no mistakes could be rectified.

But since he was playing the game to the hilt, as he always would, he needed technical assistance which only Number 2 could give him. If his 'racing fairing' were to be aerodynamically perfect, he could request the use of a computer terminal for his calculations. He couldn't claim to understand the equations in the textbooks, but he could plug in values and apply the results. After all, Number 2 would be in an ideal position to monitor his calculations, which would keep *him* interested in analysing them. And except for interface problems, which might be disguised as ground turbulence, everything would have to do with pressure flows over a dynamic surface and would guide the complex three-dimensional pattern which would form his hypothetical fibreglass.

*

He spent a week working on the framework of rod which would support his imaginary coachwork, bearing bags of bolts home from the ironmonger's along with parcels of groceries and occasional scraps from the butcher for the cat.

Number 18 asked him about it one afternoon following luncheon on the Terrace, which they now shared two or three times a week. 'What is this mechanical thing you're doing?' was her exact wording; to her partner's quizzically amused expression she enlarged, 'All those nuts and bolts you carry around with you. Are you building something?'

'Not exactly. I'm modifying something.'

'What?'

'My motorcar. You remember my motorcar – when I was first looking for Number 11 some months ago, it was in regard to –'

'Oh yes. The 739/H-F forms. I remember. You mentioned your car then. Do you still have it?'

'Yes – and I'm putting a new body on it.'

'What colour?'

'I hadn't thought, actually. It'll probably be a sort of off-white.'

'That's not right for a racing car. It should be – not red; not for you. Blue. A dark blue.'

'What about a dark green?'

'That would be nice. Yes, I think a dark green. With one bronze stripe along it.'

'What makes you think it's a racing car? There isn't much room in the Village for a racing car.'

'Oh, Number 6 – everybody was talking about your facing down Number 2 and extending your track. Oh, not out in the open, of course, but everybody in the office knew about it. And then when you mentioned your car just now, it reminded me.' She twinkled innocently at him. 'Besides, I can't see *you* driving anything but a racing car. Do you ever give people rides?'

'Very rarely. Besides, it's out of operation at the moment.'

'Did something go wrong?'

'No – I can't get any petrol, and the engine's out of tune.'

'You got your forms without any problem, I hope.'

'Yes; I filled them out and passed them on to Number 8 personally a week ago.'

'And while you're waiting, you're building a new body.'

'Only a frame for it. I'm also waiting for the fibreglass from which I can form the coachwork.'

'Oh, I see. And the fibreglass is soft of off-white?'

'I think so. I doubt if it's dark green.'

'They should make it in different colours. Can you change your order?'

'I shouldn't like to try to change anything now – it would only confuse matters and delay it another six months.'

'There must be paints for it. Have you tried the Artist's Shoppe? Oh, I'd just *love* to help you paint it!'

'We can discuss that when the time comes. I'm interested now in what else everybody in your office knows about me, since my triumph over Number 2 seems to have been common knowledge.'

'Well, you're sort of the "Mystery Man" of the Village. You keep to yourself so much, and nobody seems to know much about you – except Number 2, I suppose, since he knows everything, but . . . well . . .' She lowered her voice conspiratorially. 'I heard you'd tried to leave here.' She looked away from him in embarrassment.

He cleared his throat. 'I'm afraid it's true,' he admitted. 'But I hope that won't offend you. I promise not to try to take you with me the next time.'

She blushed furiously. 'Number 6!' she said. 'You have always behaved like a gentleman before. I'm sorry I brought the subject up, and I really wish it could be dropped at this point.'

'I'm sorry,' he said. 'I trust it may never come up between us again.'

'Very well. Now about painting your car –'

'A number of inquiries will have to be made,' he said. 'The Artist's Shoppe will be one place to ask, but I don't know enough about the subject to say whether help would be advisable. It calls for research, among other things. But you shouldn't roll up your trousers before you come to the river, as they say – after all, I haven't even designed it yet.'

'The new body?'

'It'll be like a shell, actually. And it has to be properly streamlined so as not to interfere with the airflow.'

'Oh. Like a boat.'

'Yes. Or an aeroplane. Or a racing car, for that matter.'

'Can you really go fast enough on that track for this airflow business to be important?'

'Enough that it could make a measurable difference. That's why I'm doing it. I've really become interested in improving my performance.'

'What an exciting way to pass the time! Would you take me for a ride sometime when it's all together?'

He smiled. 'Perhaps. We shall have to see what modifications will need to be made. When I get it all together again I'll let you know.'

*

One afternoon when his mountings were nearly completed, he was deep in concentration beneath the bonnet readjusting his ignition timing. Somehow the tiny variables in his engine kept slipping out of tune and demanded nearly constant attention. He faintly heard a footstep outside his garage, and elected not to react.

'Good afternoon,' said Number 2's cheerful, raucous

voice at the door. 'I wasn't sure where to knock, but I don't want to come upon you unannounced.' When this overture was not answered hostilely, he followed it into the shelter, around the stripped chassis of the car to the tool bench where the mechanic stood silently wiping his hands on a piece of rag and looking at him expectantly.

'I just thought I'd stop by and see how you were getting along. When you don't come by my office to complain about something for a full week, I begin to worry about your health.'

'I'm feeling well, thanks. Except for a constant slight headache.'

'Not sinus?'

'No – eyestrain. Naturally, I'm interested in doing the best possible job on this fairing, so I've been swotting up on aerodynamics. But the equations on the curves are quite a bit beyond my mathematical ability. I've been slogging through them by slide rule, but it's not remotely satisfactory. In short, I wonder if I could borrow a good-sized calculator for a few weeks.'

'As I believe you know, we have a central computer facility here; all we could offer you would be access to a time-sharing terminal. There might be a security problem, of course.'

'I'm sure you could find some way to trust me. I'm expecting my fibreglass any day now, and it would be most frustrating not to be able to get directly to work.'

'I quite understand, Number 6. In point of fact, one reason I stopped by was to say that I hadn't had any word yet on your fibreglass order. But I can see about having a terminal brought into your . . . Where would you like it connected?'

'How big is it?'

'About as big as a breadbin.'

'My worktable. You can probably hook it to one of the television lines.'

'Have you any idea how long you'll want it?'

'No – at least a week. Will I get a short course in operating it?'

'You will be given a programmed text which will teach you in half an hour enough to let the computer teach you itself from there on. I learned from one, though it took me almost two hours. You are familiar with the basic principles involved?'

'Fundamentally. If your computer can do the work of a million competent clerks, you hire them out a score each to fifty thousand people, each of whom pays only one ten-thousandth of the cost for the whole computer's time.'

'You also have access to the machine immediately whenever you want it – never too busy to work for you. You'd want one with a visual display, I shouldn't wonder – and a light pen. That would do wonders for your designs, Number 6. You can make a rough sketch directly on the face of a cathode-ray tube, order the computer to correct every line to precisely the mathematical curve you wish either directly or by equation, and see it done at once. With another hour's practice, in fact, you might be able to run a complete three-dimensional simulation of airflow over any shape you would care to specify. I think you would find this capability a help. Unless you object to it's being an artificial replacement for something.'

'My object is an optimum design for my fairings. I use a torch to cut metal – I don't break it in my bare hands. I'll be happy to use your computer. Just as long as your computer doesn't try to use me.'

'Superstitious nonsense, Number 6. No tool is independent of the hand behind it. You would be accusing me or my staff of conspiring against you. That couldn't have been your intent, after all we've done for you.'

'Perish the thought, Number 2. I would be overjoyed to have the use of a score of your clerks for a while – especially if they're so artistic.'

'Now, I haven't said I could get you one. In fact, I don't believe I even suggested it. Well, perhaps I did suggest it. I really don't know whether it would be feasible, in view of your record – and the assorted technical problems involved. This type of unit is still very new, and they aren't really in volume production yet. But if I can arrange for one for you, I certainly shall.

'Now I may as well not cut into your afternoon any longer. I shall look into your fibreglass and test the feasibility of this terminal arrangement. I can let you know in a few days. And by the by – thank you for not starting debates with me this time.'

'My pleasure. Be seeing you.'

The braces which would support his (still hypothetical) fairing were sturdy aluminium angle irons, with half-inch primary frame members and quarter-inch secondary braces. If it seemed overly sturdy for what should be no more than a couple of hundredweight of fibreglass, he didn't think Number 2 would be unduly concerned even if he noticed. They were intricately joined, and included a few holes which served no apparent purpose. There were wing nuts on a few of the bolts which held major subassemblies together, but they were all inside the frame and well out of sight. A couple of small eyes where pulleys could hang were unnoticeable amid the neat jumble of raw metal. Jutting ends remained untrimmed, awaiting the final pattern which would be carefully developed and extensively tested for microseconds, then reassembled and retested repeatedly until it achieved theoretical perfection before it was given physical reality in the graceful curves of formed fibreglass.

The computer terminal arrived within the week, and he spent seven consecutive hours familiarising himself with its operation and capabilities. When he finally leaned back, switched it off and went out to the kitchen to make a much-belated supper, he felt fairly familiar with the device and its limitations. Apparently he could not use it to gain access to any data he had not put into it, which was to have been expected; his clerks didn't discuss their other jobs. On the other hand, it should prove more than adequate to the job at hand. To both jobs at hand, for that matter – the ostensible racing fairing and the secondary form it should be expected to take.

In the course of a long, intent afternoon he had started his second level in Terminal Operation. Visual, with the light pen, a plastic stylus with a long cord to the unit and a microswitch beneath his index finger. He had used it to leave glowing marks on the Cathode Ray Tube, then modified them by computer into exactly defined curves, and finished by drawing a rough free-hand circle on the CRT, making it into a mathematically perfect circle and bouncing it in slow motion with specified acceleration, mass and elasticity against a base line.

The next day he was able to sketch a skeleton cube and make it rotate about any axis. Before he stopped he had included centrifugal distortion and gyroscopic inertia in his spinning cube, specifying physical constants and combining axial rotations, He had discovered most of the *Handbook of Chemistry and Physics* was available from a whole reference section which was open to him after all, along with an omnilingual range of dictionaries, the *Encyclopedia Britannica* (five years out of date) and several screensful of titles he could have scanned at his leisure.

Now he was ready to start work. His mornings were still spent out and around in the Village, and among his recent acquisitions were two rolls of metal screening, so heavy that an electric van had been engaged to haul them to his workshop along with a coil of steel ribbon two inches wide and sixty feet long.

The first roll of screen was a wide-gauge net of welded wire, the type known as 'hardware cloth.' With the bracing structure mounted in the place on the chassis of his KAR, he began to form a close-fitting, roughly curved covering of this heavy screen around it, yet unattached to it. In a dozen places, then, he cut slits in the screening and pushed through sturdy steel T-brackets, their tongues eyed for mounting bolts and their bases behind the screen, and he soldered them temporarily in place.

By this time he knew roughly what the contours of his imaginary shell should be, and he prodded and levered and bent and pushed at the resistive screen until its curves approached his approximations. Then he unrolled the ribbon of steel and ran lengths of it around the heavy wire mesh shell, riveting it to the T-brackets and drawing it tight, strapping vertically and laterally around the shell to reinforce it. Then he covered the entire affair with a full wrapping of the second roll's fine-mesh windowscreen.

That was, all told, the work of twelve afternoons. He saw no reason to prolong his labours unnecessarily when he could be pressing Number 2 for further favours. His evenings were now spent chiefly with the computer terminal, animating airflows over small sections of complex curves, varying rates of flow and viscosity and adding an unlabelled factor which involved cavitation potential but could pass for air friction in the context he used it in.

And then his fibreglass arrived, like great bolts of cloth wrapped in heavy brown paper. The tall rolls stood against the wall of his workshop for two days, spurring him to finish the last set of calculations on the camber of his suddenly possible rear deck and run a final simulation of this last modification under several hypothetical conditions. Then, with carefully traced and measured templates, he set to work building the hull itself.

Over the fine screening, with gloves on his hands against the brittle glass cloth, he drew sheets of it in irregular patches which he tacked in place and covered with penetrating pungent epoxy resins. The brownish liquid soaked into each layer of matting and hardened there slowly, fixing every fibre in a tough, resilient bond. Flows of resin dripped through the fine wire mesh to dry into lumps, stalactites, ridges and strings; some he could chip off later, the rest he could ignore.

Five layers of whitish, burlap-textured matting were laid

down, and five layers of cement soaked through them to cure to final hardness in the graceful unbroken curves of unit construction.

Sanding the surface took longer than laying it down. An electric buffer among his tools adapted well to coarse sandpaper, and carried him through progressively finer grades until the whole fairing was smooth to the touch. Then dark grey-green enamel went on, and dried to a colour like a cloudy sea. It took him, from start to finish, nearly three weeks.

And then the last coat of enamel was dry, the oil had been changed and the fuel tank filled. With proper ceremony, he summoned Number 213 and together they carefully loaded the shell, sectioned for transportation to the track on to the car. Since the Village paths were too narrow to pass the vehicle with its fairing mounted, the segments were carried like pieces of a display sign tied together on the car while Number 213 walked importantly ahead with his red flag, clearing the way of staring pedestrians.

Once at the track, together they lifted the unwieldy slabs and untied the bundles of braces which hung like fasces along both sides. Number 6 bolted them into place on the coachwork while Number 213 watched, fascinated, only coming forward to help him lift sections of the fairing into place. Then Number 6 crawled about under the car tightening the mounting bolts. They would hold as long as he needed them to hold.

With the last bolts in place, he eased himself into the driver's seat and started the engine. He drove one full circuit of the track under thirty while the eight pulsing cylinders warmed and circulated the oil, then picked up speed.

Number 213 sat on the ground by the shed watching him go by every two minutes for a while, and then was gone without waiting to wave his usual *Be seeing you.*

Number 6 studied the height of the sun above the smooth and nameless sea which was one wall of his prison. The light would not begin to fail for another hour. He'd expected Number 213 to wait longer, especially since Number 2 must be most interested in what was going on now that this vast project approached its penultimate moments. No sense in wasting more petrol; he completed one more lap, then pulled into his pit stop.

With the bulk of the car shielding him from the distant television camera, he loaded a number of well-wrapped parcels into the boot of the car, crawled underneath to check a couple of connections and connect a number of small pulleys, and then topped off his fuel tank from the last can sitting in the row along one wall. The last drops went into a plastic sack concealed under the rear deck and nearly full of fifty gallons of petrol. The sack had been tucked, empty, into the space as the first layer of fibreglass went on, and into it he had transferred his hoard. Then he had spread it beneath the hardening shell and anchored it into the framework, leak-proof and electrically grounded to one long trailing cable. Now it held his long-distance fuel.

The sun had passed behind a curtain of golden clouds which were already darkening to rose and lavender as he started the engine again and purred out on to the track in the gathering dusk.

Out from among the trees and down the long grade he rolled, shifting for the turn at the bottom and cutting hard right up the hill, slowing to twenty on the hairpin curve at the top, then roaring down the track along the base of the sheer granite wall towards the lowest point of the course at the edge of the beach. The tide was approaching flood, and the sand was packed hard just beyond where the track swung left up the slope through the irregular zig-zags and cuts of the return leg of the course.

He cut the lights of the car as he drove on to the sand just at the edge of the tide, stopped the engine and climbed out. He was now in range of no camera he had found, and his best estimates gave him fifteen minutes to complete his modifications.

He got out, reaching under the shell to release three wing nuts on each side, and then rolled the sections back from the braces. These he loosened and swung to new angles, then tightened. The quarter-inch aluminium angle-irons swung out and slanted downward around the upper part of the car, bristling a dozen diagonally-cut points at thirty-degree intervals.

The fibreglass segments slid into a new configuration, still like the racing shell, but now upside down. The stern was open; he climbed back into the car, started the engine, shifted into bottom gear and eased forward into the hull.

It rocked as the weight came into it, settling into the sand. The rear wheels dug into the hard sand and pushed the shell to the edge of the water until he felt it lifted free by the wash of a wave. The next surge swung his hull a few inches to one side, then swept around the open stern and swirled about his tyres. He climbed out again to hoist the rear panels of the hull into place, fit their snug joints together and bolt them securely.

A soft glooping sound brought his head around,

instantly alert. A giant soft spheroid, a Guardian, pale in the twilight, was flobbing toward him with definite intent to investigate and interfere. He jumped back into the car and picked up one of the two spare braces he had held out for this situation. Six feet long, diagonally cut on one end, it would only be sharp enough to puncture the tough protoplastic hide of the thing if it pushed very hard.

It came wabbling across the beach as if blown by a gust of wind, rolling and bounding. He set the brace quickly against an inner angle of the chassis, and ducked in the seat as the eight-foot sphere sensed the spear before it and vaulted more than its own height to clear the car.

The leap carried it past the line of foaming breakers on the sand and brought it down in the surf a car-length beyond the ungainly craft which was now bobbing and swaying unsteadily as shallow waves lapped about it. Number 6 swung his single line of defence to face seaward as the great bubble somehow found traction in the water and skidded towards him with a draft of no more than three inches. He thrust at it with his pole and it veered sharply to bounce against the bow of his still-grounded craft.

The impact shook him from his unsteady stance in the seat. He staggered, flourishing the pole to regain his balance, until the edge of the door caught him behind his knees and he fell backward, twisting like a cat to land on his hands. The jolt knocked the wind out of him for a moment, but the Guardian's momentum had already carried it far up the beach beyond the car. Before it could slow and return, he was almost on his feet again, brushing sand from his burning palms.

The pole had fallen near him and he scrambled to pick it

up as the ungainly thing lurched towards him. His conscious thoughts were mostly for the tide, which was rising with every minute spent and would begin to float his craft without him if the Guardian detained him long enough. He braced his spear in the sand like a pygmy faced with a charging lion, and held his ground as the blundering behemoth lumbered towards him.

As it approached, it slowed. As it slowed, he pulled the spear back to a new foothold and retreated a step toward the boat behind him. The sphere hesitated, then rolled swiftly and smoothly to his landward side. There it began moving forward, slowly, inexorably, until it just touched the tip of his brace.

Holding it tentatively at bay, he clambered back into the seat on the car. The Guardian was almost behind him now. He prodded at it, standing on the seat, then dropped the pole into the hull and turned to slide down into the seat and kick the engine to life again as the Guardian lunged ferociously at the rear of the craft and bumped it forward into the rising surf with two ramming attacks.

He gunned the engine and felt the power transmission to the rigged screw begin to push against the water under his keel. His heart began to pound in rhythm with the racing pistons as he felt his boat begin to move; he glanced back to see the great sphere, pale in the twilight, charge at him and bounce again off the transom – then he felt the stern drag clear of the sand and the surging freedom of the sea was his.

The engine rumbled and roared as he shifted pressure to his foot throttle and felt the speed increase. Looking back one more time, he saw the slow-turning spheroid floating after him, falling farther behind by the minute. He took a deep breath of the exhilarating air of freedom and then almost jumped as something landed on the passenger seat to his left.

He looked down. There, already rubbing up against him, was the black cat. And there was something unusual about it – there was a harness of some kind strapped to its body, holding a small box mounted between its shoulderblades. A signalling device? He slipped it free and examined it in the light of the instrument panel lamps. The cat had been sent to follow him – but to what result? Since this device was probably still transmitting . . . He threw it towards shore as hard as he could, and gained a momentary pleasure to see it bounce off the outdistanced Guardian, harmless though the impact was.

Nevertheless the exhilaration of his escape was now allayed by an awful suspicion of betrayal. The cat was incontrovertibly there, and it had brought an unidentifiable and unexpected device to him. Yet his reaction in throwing the box away had been the obvious response – how could they have expected to track him after the cat found him? Something was not . . .

A sound very like a muffled groan seemed to come from behind him, and he twisted to look in his rear-view mirror. The Guardian was a hundred yards behind him, a dim bobbing dot in the distance; the lights of the Village twinkled around the short rocky headland which already blocked the right half (in his mirror) from view. The sound was repeated and enlarged upon, and his hearing now placed it nearby – in the stern.

Something shifted weight, and scraping, struggling sounds from the parcel-packed bilge astern held Number 6 staring with a horrible fascination into his mirror in an effort to see around the end of his car, only glancing momentarily into the darkness ahead.

Then a silhouette rose in the mirror, obscuring the lights astern, and the throbbing craft rocked slightly as a figure stood up unsteadily, holding on to the gunnel and the car's rear mudguard. Over the muffled purr of the engine and the slapping of waves against the hull rose a familiar harsh and faintly raucous voice.

'Number 6, just what do you think you're doing?'

It could only be Number 2. The driver smiled. 'Escaping,' he said.

'Well, stop it at once! I was hoping to catch you in time to dissuade you from this rash act, but I had no idea you were prepared to add kidnapping to your list of antisocial actions.' Heeding the pitching of the craft, he crawled forward over the rear deck toward the passenger seat. The cat scrambled out of the way as Number 2 threw a leg over the door and started to climb in.

'I hope you don't expect to force me to turn around now,' the driver said 'I shouldn't like to throw you overboard.'

'Dear me, no! In dealing with a professional killer such as yourself I would always exercise the greatest care. I am an administrator, not a fighter.' He settled into the other seat, holding his free hand to his head. He took it down and looked at the smeared palm. 'Oh dear – I seem to have cut myself. I don't suppose you have a clean rag?'

'What are you doing here?'

'Being kidnapped, I believe.'

'You stowed away in my boat and remained hidden all the time I was trying to launch it? And adding ten stones to the weight, while you were at it. I don't intend to feed you for a week either, by the way.'

'I did not stow away, Number 6; I acted entirely out of concern for you. You had started down the track and failed to return. You could have been lying in a flaming tangle of metal at the foot of some gradient. I came down with the cat, and sent it ahead to look for you. When I came out on the beach, I saw you were engaged in combat with the Guardian. As I think I said, I am not a fighter – I stayed on the far side of this . . . ah . . . boat and came up just as you were thrown from it. Then I thought – well, I must admit I thought I might be able to prevent your hasty, thoughtless departure from us until I could beg for another chance to redress whatever wrongs you may feel you have suffered.

'Then, as I started to climb in over that side, the Guardian or you jostled the thing. Or it may have been a wave. But I fell, and I think I hit my head on something down here. And when I was able to sit up again, we were already well away from the shore. And here we are.'

There was silence for several seconds over the ceaseless sweeping sounds of their passage. 'Do you expect me to believe that?'

'There is it – your belief and disbelief will not alter the facts a whit. And the fact remains that I am being carried away from the Village against my will.'

'And mine. But under the circumstances, you may understand my reluctance to put about. I assure you, I intend to set you ashore at the earliest opportunity.'

'Surely, Number 6, you can't expect to succeed in this mad adventure!'

'*The scheme is rash and well may fail, but ours are not the hearts that quail, the hands that shrink, the cheeks that pale in hours of need,'* he sang. 'And you can stop calling me Number 6 now – we're past the three-mile limit. You know my name – what's yours?'

'Number 6, this is insane. I insist – '

The engine died. Easily, quietly, with one feeble kick, the engine died. The boat lurched as it lost way, and veered slightly to port with the breeze from land.

Number 6 pressed the starter, and the electric motor under the bonnet whined and strained, but the engine did not fire. It was though the ignition were switched off. He kept trying to start, varying manipulation of the foot throttle and choke until they were dead in the water, drifting gently with the ebbing tide, and the great silence of the sea rose around them.

Even Number 2's rasping voice seemed somehow hushed, if none the less indignant. 'Now look what you've got us into! And you don't even have a radio in this thing – how will anyone find us?'

'At least you admit they're looking. You should also know better than I how they will find us. Infrared seems most likely, though I imagine the metal of the car would stand out to radar.'

'You continually assume that I know everything. There is a great deal of ocean, Number 6 – we shall probably have to spend at least one night and day in this cockleshell before we're rescued. I trust your hospitality will extend over that period, especially considering the consequences if you are found without me.'

'You're an important figure, Number 2 – surely the

Village will not let you spend an unsheltered night at sea with a homicidal madman.'

'Come, come – you're putting words in my mouth. I never implied that you killed thoughtlessly or needlessly – merely professionally. You seem to have a great deal of guilt concealed around that subject, you know – really far too much. And the feeling is perfectly normal for someone with an upbringing like yours – the conflicting concepts of your ingrained moral ethos telling you your patriotic duty and your human responsibilities were irreconcilably opposed, and you opted for the easy path, the selfish path. And you kept it up as long as you could, knowing it was wrong, hating yourself more with every death on your conscience. Because only the first two were really hard. The third was almost easy, and the fourth was meaningless. It seemed strange how casually you could become accustomed to snuffing out human life.' Number 2's voice remained cool and clinical. He did not look at his subject.

'But of course you couldn't keep it up forever – no one could and still remain remotely sane. You have a remarkable instinct for self-preservation; your resignation came just before you were to have been ordered to Argentina.'

'I would really rather hear *your* life story, Number 2 – I know my own fairly well. Up until last summer, I should say; portions since then have been somewhat confused. But you could tell me about that, too, couldn't you. You may as well – if you'll pardon my saying so, we're in the same boat and likely to remain so for several hours at least. I don't play cards, I am not fond of word games, riddles, or ghost stories. But I dote on detailed reminiscences. Tell me your life story, Number 2, since you already know mine. What has brought you to this place, at this time?'

'This is really –'

'Start at the beginning. Leave nothing out. No, you can omit your primary schooling – it's written all over you.'

'My school, it may interest you to know, took your school at rugger three years out of four while I was there.'

'Ah. So you were three years ahead of me.'

'No – five. Look! Over there!'

Sweeping spotlights fanned out from a distant power launch bearing towards them, and the stutter of the diesels carried faintly over the intervening waves.

'*At least a night and a day*, I believe you said? Really, Number 2, you underestimate your own minions. Why, it's hardly been half an hour. You've been marvellous at helping pass the time, but I'm afraid I can't afford to wait . . .' He stood up on the seat. 'You can keep the car – there's land about a mile away, and I intend to try for it.'

'Against the tide? You'd never make it. I'm almost embarrassed to have to curtail your dramatic gesture, but I feel I should point out there is a Guardian directly beneath you, and whichever way you swim, it will bring you back here and keep you here until the Rescue Unit arrives. So why not leave your shoes on and save yourself a useless drenching?'

The glare of the searchlight splayed him against the darkness like a projected image before he dropped back into the seat and heaved an almost inaudible sigh.

Nothing further was said until the launch pulled alongside them and dropped a ladder. An amplified voice echoed over them: '*Stand by to be taken in tow. Would you care to come aboard?*' A rope sailed over the side in a flying coil to drape ten slack feet across the bonnet and the far gunnel. '*Make it fast,*' the voice advised, and Number 2 scrambled over the windscreen to obey.

Number 6 stood, and looked over the side of his captured boat. The black waters could have concealed a fleet of submarines, and very likely did hold at least one animate spheroid, but he had little to lose. He rose to his feet as Number 2 stooped out of sight to secure the hawser to his front bumper, braced his hands on the edge of the door and took two deep breaths.

As he lifted one foot to the edge, the waters below him rolled silently in the moonlight and a ghostly pale shape appeared just below the surface, almost brushing his keel. He let out this third breath and replaced his foot on the seat. He would call a bluff, but could also recognise a lost hand and fold it to await the next deal.

'*Number 6,*' repeated the amplified voice, '*would you care to come aboard?*'

Number 2 stood up and waved at the launch which rose and fell gently beside them. 'Yes, certainly,' he called back. 'We'll be right there. I think this is snug . . . er, belayed.'

He squeezed between the side of the car and the hull toward where a short ladder came down from the bigger boat. 'Aren't you going to "give up the ship," captain?' he asked Number 6. 'Or do you prefer to ride back into port on the end of a towrope?' He waited a few seconds, then shrugged and turned to the launch. 'Go ahead,' he called up to the shadowed deck. 'We'll follow you in.'

The mutter of the twin diesels deepened its pulse and the launch moved slowly ahead of them, easing into the slack of the towrope as Number 2 flopped into the passenger seat again. 'Really, Number 6, you can't expect just to keep sitting there. You have taken absolutely no part in your own rescue; you refuse the hospitality of your rescuers and obviously do not intend to thank them.'

'I don't really feel they deserve my thanks. As for going aboard your yacht, I frankly feel safer in a boat I built myself.'

'*Our* engines don't just die, Number 6. No, you hate to give up your role, even though your one-and-a-half-ton twenty footer isn't much of a prize at the moment. You are too sensitive to the trappings of power, I think – even when you have relinquished effective command you cling to your position as Captain of the Good Ship . . . What is her name, by the way? I don't recall the launching ceremonies too clearly.'

'This thing? You accuse me of clinging to a title, but you seem to be more prone to labelling things. My boat, my cat – do you expect me to have pet names for my shirts as well?'

'It's considered a normal human trait to anthropomorphise certain types of things – perhaps I had forgotten you are less prone to "normal human traits" than most of us. Labels may not be as necessary to you as to me; labels are tools for communication, and you seem reticent to the point of taciturnity, especially when you suspect me of something. You seem almost afraid to speak during times of emotional stress. You are a lonely man, Number 6. You hold yourself apart from everything. Why? Why, Number 6?'

The roar of engines eased ahead of them, and they slowed as the rope went slack. The launch began backing water, taking up the line. Moments later the amplified voice spoke again across the moonlit water. '*Number 2, stand by to come aboard.*'

Making a trumpet of his hands with one elbow braced over the top of the windscreen, Number 2 called, 'Thank you, no – I'm quite comfortable here.'

'*We are taking you aboard, Number 2. There is an important call for you.*'

'It can wait.'

The stern of the launch drew alongside them, this time on the port side, a short rope ladder dangling beside Number 2.

'I think they want you to go aboard,' said Number 6.

'Well – it is chilly out here . . . Will you come if I do, Number 6? Please? Your boat will be in the safest of hands. I'll go first and you can pass the cat up to me.'

'The cat? Where is the cat?'

'I thought you had him. Well, he couldn't have gone overboard. Perhaps he jumped to the launch while I was attaching the towrope. Now come along up like a good fellow. I'm sure you'll have that engine running like a watch in no time – and it'll stay that way as long as it doesn't come too near the water, I promise you.'

Reluctantly, facing the inevitable, with patience and fortitude, he stood and followed Number 2, spurning the extended hand and climbing the four wooden slats alone.

As the launch picked up speed slowly to tauten the tow with professional smoothness, a glowing television screen in the main cabin showed a face which one of the two castaways recognised.

'Number 4 – thank you for getting this launch out to us so –'

'I am the new Number 2. You are, effective as of this moment of notification and pending full investigation, Number 100.'

Number 100's face went slack. 'You – you cannot assume this authority without . . . without confirmation! This is unprecedented!'

'Not at all. You assumed your recent post when our beloved Number 6 defected, pending full investigation which later proved you justified. As for my designation, officially I am Two Prime. But my friends,' he added meaningfully, 'call me Number 2.'

Number 100 seemed staggered. 'But – but on what grounds can you possibly base this impossible action?'

'Their full extent has yet to come to light. But the most obvious include conspiracy, assorted charges of treason and attempting unauthorised departure by stealth.'

'And piracy,' Number 6 suggested.

'This is impossible! I was kidnapped! Number 6 – you will admit you did not receive my aid in your suicidal scheme; I was trying to dissuade him from it when – '

'Save your defence for the hearing, Number 100. If anything Number 6 might say could be admitted as evidence, use will be made of him. You are remanded to the custody of the Rescue Unit – Number 77, you will follow the usual procedure.' And the screen went dark.

As it did there was some trouble in the stern, and the launch seemed to lose way. Another voice called, 'Slow! She's sprung a leak!'

Number 6 hurried back to the rail in time to see his craft,

his days and months of work and care, his hour of freedom, yawing fiercely at the end of a hawser, nosing down sluggishly in the swells and rolling with them.

'She's shipping water,' said someone in a natty cap. 'I don't know how long we can keep her afloat.'

Number 100's voice was at his elbow, subdued, bitter. 'So we have both lost that which we most prized, that which represented our greatest labours. You could have driven happily on your track. You didn't have to take your beautiful car out to sea in your perishing fibreglass sieve – and now you're going to lose it in fifty fathoms of salt water!'

'Seven fathoms, sir,' said someone. 'We're only a mile or so out now.'

'We may have to cut it loose,' said someone else. 'It seems to be going all to pieces. Looks like the towing is too much strain on the hull.'

The power launch lost way and the towrope dipped back into the water. 'Can we keep it afloat?' asked one of the crew. 'It'll hold us like a sea-anchor as fast as it goes under.'

'Keep a steady thousand RPM,' said Number 77. 'We'll take it in as far as we can.'

The rope lifted taut, and stretched to drag the nose of the wallowing derelict momentarily clear of the waves which threatened to swamp it. But the prow barely rose before lurching forward again, and they could feel the sudden drag on the launch.

'Stand by to release tow,' said Number 77. 'Sorry, Number 6, but we can't possibly make it in with the dragging. If we had flotation chambers we could buoy it up, but . . .'

'Number 2, you could order a Guardian to come up under it.'

'I am not Number 2, I am Number 100; I cannot order myself a sandwich, let alone a Guardian; we are well inside the ring of submerged stations and the things aren't that manoeuvrable under water; and a ton or more would crush it directly back to the bottom, since they have only a few hundred pounds practical buoyancy. Other than these minor objections, your idea was a nice bit of creative thinking.' Number 100's voice betrayed his bitterness.

The launch continued to slog toward shore, pausing and lunging against its load as the waves gripped and released the sinking hulk. Ahead the lights of shore danced on the waters, and a white line of surf rose and fell in the moonlight against the dark deserted strand.

'It's going under.' called someone from the flying bridge, and Number 77 said regretfully, 'We'll have to cut it loose, Number 6. There's no way we could get it back to shore now.'

'Could you float a marker over it?' asked Number 6.

'Certainly. Perhaps it could be salvaged.'

His craft was now obviously beyond saving – it settled in the water even as he watched. The launch reversed as a crewman tied a yellow plastic can to a line, and they came alongside as wavelets began slopping over the thwarts. Cold, dark, corrosive seawater was lapping around the blind headlamps and almost to the tops of the doors. As a crewman leaned over to affix the marker buoy and sever the towrope, Number 6 turned from the rail into the darkness of the deck.

Moments later the twin screws resumed their mutter and

in the white noise of the wash astern he could not distinguish the slow, sucking gurgle of water surging over the sides of a sinking coracle. In his mind he concentrated on a single point – it had gone down dead level. He'd had it balanced precisely. Next time . . .

*

Number 77 conducted him directly to his flat and saw him in. When he had gone, Number 6 tried the front door. It was immovable, as was the kitchen door. He picked up his telephone handset.

'Number 4,' he said.

There was a pause. 'That Number has been changed, sir. You are calling Number 2 . I will connect you.'

In a moment his television screen glowed to life. 'I was expecting you to call directly, Number 6,' he said. 'First, I must apologise for the loss of your construction. We understand your emotional state of involvement with it, and are prepared to make it up to you. However, I am afraid you will not find me as approachable as my predecessor; your requests to me must pass through the proper channels. You will no longer be able to walk into my office at will.'

'I shall miss those excellent tea-biscuits. The baker doesn't stock them, you know.'

'He may if properly approached. But you will be expected to behave yourself in the future, Number 6, or shortages may be expected to appear in various stocks.'

'Behave myself? Number 2 , I intend to leave you undisturbed as soon as I have your permission to salvage my car. I will need at least a set of diving apparatus, two flotation chambers and a boat of some kind. I can do the job myself, and you can watch me every minute to your heart's content. I will shortly want a wagon, or truck, capable of carrying the salvage to my workshop.'

Number 2 stared out of the screen at him.

'Let's not bump heads, Number 2 . I don't know what I could find to keep me occupied if I were to become overwrought with the loss of all those months of work. But I'm afraid my feelings toward the Village in general and yourself in particular are not especially *mutual* at the moment.'

'Without your euphemisms, are you phrasing a threat?'

'Yes. I want my car back. I am willing to do all the work, but I can't do it barehanded and I will risk a great deal to get the tools for the job.'

'You wouldn't dare cause too much trouble. You have already come closer than you know to neutralisation. With the slightest effort I could have you converted to Number 406, with your entire personality reduced to so much suet. How would you feel about pushing a broom the rest of your life, Number 6? I can tell you now that you wouldn't mind it – you wouldn't mind much of anything after a few weeks of re-education so you could feed and dress yourself. Now have dinner and go to bed. Tomorrow buy yourself a needlework set and forget about your sunken treasure.'

'Tomorrow evening I will be comfortably in bed when your Green Dome catches fire and burns to the ground. Or I can start picking off your television cameras, one by one. Or I may even go out hunting Guardians with a sharp stick. Or distributing revolutionary pamphlets in the Village

Square. Because I don't think you dare to damage me permanently. You are still only Two Prime, and I can tell you right now that I intend to call your bluff. I'll even wager that I could force you to destroy me against your will, and I really don't think you can afford to let that happen. All I want is an opportunity to salvage what I can, subject to the conditions already stated. Your investment and risk will be small.'

Number 2 remained carefully expressionless. 'We will have to take your proposal under advice, Number 6. There is no precedent . . .'

'There are countless precedents for Villagers working on their own projects with Village help. As for thinking it over, every minute under the water means more damage to my engine. Tomorrow I must start devoting my full effort to one cause or the other – if I can't raise my car, then I will raise the very devil!'

'Don't push it, Number 6. There is no way you could start this . . . project tonight. Withhold your violent reprisals until tomorrow, at the least. It's late. Everyone is in bed.'

'I will call for your final word at nine in the morning. Silence will be taken to mean refusal.'

'Number 6, you don't seem to care for other people's problems. You are also dangerously peremptory for someone in your position.'

'That may be – if you have any punishment you think will be effective under the circumstances, I invite you to try it. If I haven't heard from you by nine tomorrow morning, I'll call for your decision. Be seeing you.' And so saying, he rang off.

Only then, as he walked out to the kitchen, did he realise his knees were shaking slightly. True visceral anger was a rare experience to him, and he found it less than pleasant. It was deeper and harder to direct than the cold intellectual anger which drove him night and day; it became dangerously elemental.

As he prescribed himself a stiff drink and dinner, he realised he had also come closer than he liked to admit to losing his temper. Even so, his decision stood logically. There would inevitably come a time, sooner or later, when he would have to force the Village to reveal itself or destroy him. Or free him. And now was as good a time as any.

A faint sound from the back door attracted his attention, and he put his ear to the panel. The cat seemed to be outside, meowing for admittance. He tried the latch, but it was still immovable. So he was locked in and the cat was locked out, at least until morning. Maybe they would keep him imprisoned here until they decided his violent period had passed.

He refilled his glass as he returned to the living room. A cold draught made him turn in time to see the kitchen door closing silently as the black cat stepped unhurriedly over the threshhold. When he tried the latch manually ten seconds later, it was again fixed.

One of the lessons the Village had taught him was patience in the face of helpless frustration – he did not even scowl as he refilled his glass and returned to the living room. The cat was standing in his chair, kneading the cushion with its forepaws. As he approached, it sprang lightly to the arm of the chair and balanced as he seated himself. It looked over its shoulder at him, then stepped carefully into his lap, one foot at a time. He rested his free hand on its head, and it butted up into his palm and began to purr. He was hardly aware of the distant sounds of London, muffled by the rain outside his windows, as he dozed in the armchair for half an hour before going to bed.

*

At precisely 9:00 by the tower bell, his front door chime sounded. Number 94 lounged against the doorpost, clipboard and ballpoint in hand; in the back of his electric truck were five bulky parcels.

'Number 2 gave me to understand you would be ready at nine o'clock,' he said. 'I'm to run you and your gear down to the beach and stand by if you want any help.'

'I'll appreciate the lift – you can probably bring me back here when I've looked over the job and found out what tools I'll need.' He ran a mental checklist – lights, stove, windows – as he drew the door to and felt it latch.

He squatted in the back examining his loot during the cobblestoned ride down winding Village paths, while Number 94 tooted at passers-by. There were three military surplus self-inflating liferafts, all still packaged; one had rowlocks and oars. All three opened automatically when water dissolved a protected seal. The fourth and fifth bundles were a complete wet suit with accoutrements and two fully charged tanks of air. He leaned forward and addressed the driver. 'Number 94 –'

'Oh, he said the wagon would be ready when you are; I can bring it down to the beach for you.'

'Thank you, but I'll only want you to run me back to my

place and make a stop or two after I make a preliminary dive. I probably shan't want the wagon until past noon.'

They parked two of the collapsed rubber rafts against the seawall, and Number 94 was set down to guard them. From the beach Number 6 could see the bright marker buoy, a yellow fleck against a grey-green sea. His first job would be to dive down to the wreck and study its position. If the bottom was firm and the wreck easily accessible from all sides as he hoped, he could have it afloat quickly and hope that the lubricants in the engine had afforded adequate protection during the immersion.

The bathing machines were vacant at this hour – he took the wet suit into the nearest and emerged twelve minutes later wearing the dull black second skin. He hoisted the third raft with its oars under his arm and strolled boldly down the beach.

Knee-deep in the gentle waves, he shifted the oars to his left arm and tossed the rubber packet twenty feet out, beyond the edge of the surf. In seconds it grew, sections popping and puffing to full firmness as he splashed out to clamber into it.

Unshipping the oars, he rose to his knees on the rubber mid-seat and squinted across the water to sight the marker buoy nearly half a mile out from the shore in thirty feet of water. The sky was bright and the water clear – considering the depth, he could probably have done the job without the compressed air, but it would have taken longer. And time was his worst enemy now.

It took ten minutes to scull out to the marker; when he made the rubber raft fast to it he adjusted the belt of weights around his waist, took the mouthpiece between his teeth and drew a lungful of cool stale air before setting the mask down over his face and rolling backwards off the edge.

He sank slowly feet first. As the bubbles cleared around him he saw the line a few feet away extending down to a dark shape beneath him. He gripped the rope and accelerated his movement downward, swaying lightly to the faint regular surge of the water past the float above, feeling the soft fist of pressure squeezing his chest.

He swallowed hard to clear his ears and blew a little water out of the mouthpiece as he neared the bottom. There the derelict lay, still pointed toward shore, scarely a drift of sand around the wheels of the drowned car which still stood squarely amid a bare wire-mesh framework.

He squinted through the dimness. Yes, the wires were bare. The painstakingly applied, supposedly impervious fibreglass they had sold him seemed to have dissolved in the seawater. It had been formed and solidified around that wire mesh, and soaked with 'epoxy resin' – either it had totally dissolved or they had substituted an absolutely perfect replica of his frame, complete with a shimmering, quivering mass in the frame of the rear deck: fifty gallons of petrol still trapped in a tough plastic bag.

He studied the position of the car on the sea floor – and then noticed the floor itself, which not only bore no vegetation and concealed no visible marine life, but which, except for a slight wash of sand here and there, was not quite as smooth and clean as the floor of a swimming pool.

The bottom was hard, so his first plan still looked best. But his salvage scheme changed slightly; instead of taking everything with him this afternoon, he would leave the hull framework behind along with anything that would not be damaged by another day's immersion. he wanted an excuse to come back later and study this eerily empty world. A barrier somewhere must keep out the omnipresent life of the sea; even if this unnaturally bare floor gave no foothold for anchoring life-forms, there should have been plankton and fish.

Now every minute his engine spent under water meant added hours of labour before he could drive it again. He had finished his evaluation; the last details of his plan came clear in his mind as he shot back up the long rope from where his car waited on the bottom.

*

Number 94 was lounging in the morning sunshine on top of the sea wall with his straw hat over his eyes as Number 6 splashed ashore, dragging his raft up the sand above the line of the surf. He paused to shed his weights and tanks and replace his flippers with unstockinged trainers, then trotted up to the electric cart. 'Back to my place,' he ordered. 'I'll need a few things. And I want to stop by the Ironmonger's – I have a few quick purchases to make.'

The cart hummed to a halt under the tree by the Village smithy, and Number 6 stepped out on to the bricks. Inside the shop Number 26 stood to greet him.

'I want about a hundred and fifty feet of quarter-inch cable and a dozen – no, two dozen thimbles.'

'You're certainly the busy one,' said the shopkeeper. 'Always a project going.' He found the heavy cable-cutters and crossed to the racked drums of ropes and cables.

'That's a lot of cable – building a suspension bridge?' He chuckled at his own pleasantry.

'No,' said his customer succinctly. 'I'm floating a sunken ship.'

'Do tell!' the other marvelled. 'Well, I've got about a hundred and twenty or thirty feet left here on this one – would that do? I could cut into another roll for you if you want, but I'd sooner not.'

'One hundred and twenty or thirty will be fine; I'd sooner have it spooled. You can put all this on my account, of course – and here is a sack for the thimbles.' Number 26 counted out the small, U-shaped bolts, threaded on both legs with a bar bolted between them. 'Fine – be seeing you.'

Back in the electric cart, lugging a massive spool of cable under one arm, Number 6 said, 'Now go directly round to my workshop. I'll just need to pick up a couple of tools.'

Still slightly clumsy in the wet suit, he padded into his garage and spent most of a minute finding a ratchet socket wrench to fit the nuts on the thimble he held and a bolt-cutter capable of shearing quarter-inch cable. He also cut two lengths of twine four feet long and six inches of heavy insulating tape and took them all with him back to the cart.

'Now – back to the beach, and you can help me carry a few things.'

As they drove, he busied himself fashioning the two lengths of twine into safety lines from both the socket wrench and the bolt-cutter to his belt. He was done and satisfied by the time they arrived at the foot of the cement ramp.

There were a few people on the beach by now, since it was past 10:00 o'clock, but none of them paid much attention to the unnumbered man in the black wet suit and his sportily dressed assistant carrying things down to the surf near the south end of the beach. They loaded the heavy spool of cable into the raft, which sagged alarmingly but held; added a heavy paper sack and two dull rubber bundles and a pair of large hand-tools on cords. Then with less help from Number 94, who didn't want to get his shoes wet, the raft was set afloat again.

Number 6 spent the next ten minutes rowing back out to the marker buoy and anchoring there again. For half an hour he worked with cable and cutters, thimbles and wrench.

Measuring the cable off the spool in double-arm-spreads like a drapery assistant clerk, he formed a loop of twelve feet and clipped it with three thimbles. The U-shaped bolts fitted over the paired cables and had a crossbar tightened down over the open end by two nuts which could be tightened in seconds with the socket wrench in his other hand. The closed ends of the thimbles passed around the short side of the loop; the long side ran out twelve feet more to its free end. He made four of these, then tossed them over the side.

Last, he carefully tore the insulating tape into four pieces and stuck two of them over the soluble seal on each of the uninflated rafts. Then he untied the cable-cutters from his belt and attached them to a loop on the raft, adjusted his mask and mouthpiece, and rolled the paper bag, which now contained a dozen thimbles, tightly to squeeze excess air out. He gripped it around the wrench in his left hand, clamped his right over his mask to secure it, and rolled himself backwards over the side.

His four loops of cable lay half draped over the hulk of his car and its open-work hull. He started at once with the first loop, threading its free end around the nearest wheel, looping it snugly and clamping it with three more thimbles, his socket wrench tightening the nuts in quick, bright arcs. He moved to the next wheel, took the nearest free end of the cable and did it all again. In ten minutes he had all four placed and connected, working with a fierce concentration in the dim light, soundless save for the drumming of his blood in his ears, the preternaturally sharp muffled clicks of his wrench and the alternate thunder and hiss of his slow, regular breathing.

Then back to the surface, pausing halfway up to swallow and yawn as well as possible through a demand valve. He stuck his head and an arm over the edge of the bobbing raft just long enough to grab the two rubber parcels, then doubled over and surface-dived, clutching them both in his arms. They fought the descent, but he kicked steadily downward, breathing more rapidly until he reached the bottom again. There, gripping one package between his knees, he knotted the handrope of the other around the near front loop of cable. That temporarily secured, he let it bob up and took the other to the other side. There he drew both large loops of cable together around the raft and tied the handrope around both of them, arranging the raft so that when it opened, it would be upside down within the loops. Then, both hands freed, he went back and did the same with the first.

Now all was in place. He took off the handbrake, then bent to the nearer raft. He picked at the tape over the soluble seal with a fingernail until a corner came free, then pulled at it. In seconds the bundle began to unfold, slowly, because of the water pressure. As it did so, he swam around to the other and removed its seal as well. The irregular thuds of collapsed sections opening out beat against his eardrums as the compressed CO_2 fought the weight of the water to a compromise. They wouldn't be able to inflate fully under an atmosphere and a half, but they would buoy the weight enough for him to lift it. Submerged, it couldn't have a dead weight of much over five hundred pounds, and if he could once get it moving upward the rafts would begin to expand and increase their lift until he might be in danger of being sucked to the surface so quickly he could burst a lung.

When the second raft started to inflate, he swam back to the first. Bracing his feet against the sides of the car, he manhandled the flabby, struggling lump of rubber-trapped gas until it was roughly centred in its two loops of cable and hung half-folded, like a doughy pup-tent sagging upward as it continued to grow slowly.

Then back to the second raft. Already half-inflated, it had not fallen into the correct position. The aft cable was too close to the centre and slipping forward. More expanding gas swelled the larger end, threatening to pull free of its harness.

He kicked once and was above the wreck, already rocking with the lift of the under-inflated rafts. Taking the loop of the cable in both hands, he drove his legs downward into the dense, springy mass of the float. Dragging the cable astern over the quivering evasive surface, he snagged it around a handhold two thirds of the way back and got his fingers out of the way as he let it down gently and kicked free. It looked as if it should hold.

The wreck was almost ready to lift free of the seabed. It took many seconds to pick apart the water-swollen knot that held the marker buoy line to the bumper and refasten it to the hull frame. This done, he swam under one tentlike inverted raft and allowed a few cubic feet of his exhalation bubbles to collect in it, then swam around to the other and repeated the action.

It was stirring now – once it started up, it would accelerate as the water pressure decreased and the swelling rafts displaced more and more. He crouched cautiously by the front bumper, steadied himself, and lifted. It wasn't heavy, but it was massive. It gave perceptibly – it swayed and rose and he felt his legs straighten as the huge affair rocked and drew up, floating slowly at first, then falling away from him faster to soar gracefully into the light-hazed reaches of the upper depths above.

Suction pulled about him, but he clung to the framework until the dusty mirror of the surface far above shattered to greenish-white. Then he took a breath, opened his throat and kicked off for the top. Air surged from his lungs in an endless rush, expanding freely as he shot towards the daylight above. He was still ten feet below the dark cloud of his salvage structure when his lungs were empty, and he kicked twice more before his head broke the surface and he gulped cool fresh air along with a few droplets of spray.

He scrambled aboard his raft and shed the mask, weights, flippers and tank. There was half an hour's air left, and he had other uses for it. He sculled his raft around to shoreward off the car, which rode half-submerged between the bulky faded-orange waterwings that bracketed it, then pulled ten more feet of cable from the nearly empty spool.

After anchoring the drum securely around a stern cleat in the raft, he made the free end fast to the bumper half a yard beneath the surface, leaning over the comfortably soft and sun-warmed rubber stern. Then he picked up the oars and began a slow steady stroke towards shore, just stirring the great mass that hung in the water behind him.

It was more than half an hour until, palms worn half raw and forearms throbbing, he felt the suck and slide of the surf behind him. He rested his oars and twisted on the seat, feeling his spine crack, to look over his shoulder.

It was nearly noon, and the tide was almost out. For a wonder, Number 94 had been paying attention. The promised wagon was waiting, with block and tackle and a small windlass, on the hardpacked sand at the edge of the surf.

He turned again to his oars with a different stroke. Now he pulled with the lift of each wave and fought its draw until he felt the scrape and drag of his burden brushing the sandy bottom. If the wheels still turned . . .

Another swell lifted it, and he pulled twice on the oars and gained five feet before his load grounded and bumped – and rolled. He shipped the oars and took the cable spool. Rising to his knees, he shook the last loops free and tossed it, unreeling, toward the shore from the peak of the next wave. Number 94 caught it and connected the bare end to the windlass.

In fifteen minutes the car was lashed to the low sturdy frame of the wagon behind the heaviest-duty electric cart available in the Village. The tower clock had not yet chimed the hour of 1:00 when it was let down again in front of

Number 6's workshop. White crusts of salt rimed the drying body.

Without removing his wet suit, Number 6 connected the garden hose to the houseside tap and turned it on his car. That salt had to be washed off as quickly as possible and fresh water was the best way since its corrosive effect would be miniscule compared to that of the seawater. His KAR had been under water less than eighteen hours – if the lubricating oil hadn't dissolved, he could still save the engine, though he would have to disassemble it and clean it piece by piece. The engine should have had time to cool off before the sinking, so the block might still be sound. And still the challenge remained to determine what conditions were result and which cause of the unexplained failure of his engine. Only the symptoms he'd observed had given any clue . . .

'Number 6 – what about the rest of your junk? Your diving gear – and all those rafts you left lying on the beach?' Number 94 stood by the electric cart, watching him disinterestedly.

'They're well above the tide line. I shall want them tomorrow when I go down to bring up the hull frame. If you would be good enough to leave my things here – yes, right there will be fine – and call for me tomorrow morning at ten. I shall finish my salvage project and clear the area. Mind the hose!'

'Sorry. Good afternoon, Number 6 – ten o'clock.'

'Be seeing you.'

He spent the next two hours working steadily. The KAR had to be put up on blocks so the wheels could be removed; the engine had to be laid open and stripped to its component elements. Bearings had to be extracted, washed, inspected minutely, carefully re-oiled and re-assembled. Only the washing and drying must be done this afternoon – the rest of it could easily take him a few weeks. Possibly even many weeks. And what would happen then would depend on what happened before then.

*

The next morning he heard the 10:30 chime faintly across the water from shore as he made his raft fast to the bobbing yellow marker buoy above the spot where he hoped the framework of his craft still lay, unless the aluminum bracing and steel screening had dissolved overnight as his 'fibreglass' had.

He checked the tanks again – about half an hour's air. Skip breathing could extend it to forty or forty-five minutes; there were no currents in this sterile sea and nowhere he could go too deep to return to the surface on his last lungful of air. He flushed his lungs with the last free oxygen he'd have until his bottled supply ran out or he found what he was looking for – and since he didn't know what he was looking for, the former seemed more likely. At any rate, he would have time to finish, dry and dress before lunch. Clamping a hand over his mask and gripping the mouthpiece between his teeth, he rolled backwards off the edge of the raft.

He came out of the roll head down and stroked for the bottom, drawing a long deep breath as he shot into the green immensities below and the light faded above him. There was the framework of his hull – the shore was *that* way – the first thing to do would be head straight out to seek the boundary that kept the infinitely viable life of the sea from this small bay.

Arms straight to his sides, legs straight and kicking smoothly, six feet above the bottom he bored through the unresisting water into featureless obscurities. Breathing in sips, holding each for ten seconds; *kick-kick-kick-kick-kick-kick-kick-kick(breathe)kick-kick-kick-kick-kick-kick-kick-kick(breathe)* . . . Wisps and curls of sand slid silently by beneath him, the only visible indication of his progress. Minutes passed. He must have been a mile from shore when something else appeared dimly ahead of him – a silent pale shape, large and indistinct.

As it approached, he forgot to release his last breath. Twenty feet away in the eerie green twilight he could make out the quivering, gelatinoid blob of a Guardian under pressure. It had compressed irregularly, like a half-empty balloon, in huge wrinkles which shifted and rippled like wind-driven grass as it fought through the water towards him, somehow maintaining a neutral buoyancy against all natural tendencies.

He couldn't distinguish its exact colour through the water – whether it was a killer or a herder. Since it was less likely to encounter Villagers down here than invading sea life, it was more likely to be a scavenger of anything organic that came beyond the beach and the proper swimming area. It wasn't a hunter; its movements were too slow, even as it seemed to sense him and start vaguely towards him. He twisted in the water and kicked away from it, leaving a cloud of exhaled bubbles fluttering upwards out of sight.

So the floor of this doubtful ocean was not left

unwatched after all. Nor was it totally deserted, since the presence of the Guardian presupposed a need for it. But there was no evidence it had ever been called up to function before – for that matter, he couldn't even be certain it had sensed him before he stirred away from it.

He had taken off at roughly a right-angle to his left, which meant he should be paralleling the shore towards the headland to the south of the Village. It stuck most of a hundred yards from the beach, so he should pass well seaward of it, but for the fact that it marked the southern boundary of the Village. Whatever defence preserved this shallow bay most likely came to land there. When he reached it, he could follow it in.

He swam swiftly, efficiently. *Kick-kick-kick-kick-kick-kick-kick-kick(breathe)kick-kick-kick-kick-kick-kick-kick-kick(breathe)* . . . His eyes scanned the visible area of the bottom for cracks, fissures, jetsam or any markings besides the endless calligraphy of lightly drifted sand constantly rewritten by gentle currents across the bottom. There was no evidence of any barrier at the surface – he must have been well beyond the Village boundary when they'd turned him back, and he had seen nothing. How far below the surface did it end? His boat had drawn three or four feet and hadn't touched anything. What could it be?

He broke himself away from the almost hypnotic fascination of the tangled non-pattern, the rhythmic beat of his legs and shallow breathing, for a glance at his wrist-watch. He'd been swimming for seven minutes since he'd seen the Guardian – nearly half a mile. He should have come to the barrier by this time. Perhaps he had angled nearly parallel to it – without a compass directions were uncertain. He had a little more than half his air left; rather than waste it in a blind search, he kicked for the surface where he could re-orient himself.

When his head broke water, the glare of the midday sun blinded him briefly. When his eyes cleared, he could see nothing ahead of him but the foreshortened swells of the ocean. He seemed to be alone in the centre of an empty circle. With a kick and a twist, he swung about and saw his own yellow marker buoy some fifty feet away and the familiar beach and cottage-clustered hills beyond to the right. Instead of swimming parallel to the shore, he had somewhere turned farther left than he intended and wound up nearly back at his starting point.

Still, fifteen minutes of air had not been totally wasted; even negative evidence could be useful data. Now what of his other fifteen minutes? Skip-breathing would stretch it to twenty or twenty-five; he could make it to South Point and back with a little margin. If he ran dry suddenly he could finish the return on the surface. It didn't especially matter if Number 2 saw him coming *back* from the border.

He took a careful sight on the tip of the promontory where it jutted out to rocks awash with waves. Then he dived like an otter to five feet below the surface, and swam with an eye on the dancing image of the sun to keep him headed roughly south. The bottom was likely to look the same as far as he went, and the shallow depth would deplete his air supply only half as rapidly.

After five minutes, he could hear waves shattering on the rocks and grinding pebbles to sand. The sound was peculiarly sharp and insistent, as all underwater sounds are; it guided him as it grew and the featureless plane beneath him rose and began to sprout natural-looking protuberances.

Now the waves were beginning to pull at him; he bore to the right away from them and noticed it was beginning to become slightly harder to breathe. Only about ten minutes of air left. If he used the last breath in the tanks on this quest, he would have to salvage his fifty gallons of petrol and the steel-and-aluminium framework which could still prove the key to his escape by free diving, which did not particularly appeal to him. He could hold out here for another five minutes and go back entirely on the surface, which meant much more work, and still have enough underwater time left to drop the ballasted keel which held the hulk to the bottom.

Where was he now? The endless applause of the rocks was behind him, the floor out of sight below. He angled downward and away from the shore. And there was something on the bottom – dark, and round . . . He stroked downward, feeling air force itself into his open lungs to balance the growing pressure on his ribs.

It wasn't something – it was a hole. A hole, six or more feet across – apparent sizes are deceptive underwater. He couldn't see its sides, or anything inside.

Then he heard another sound, building – a rush and burbling roar as of volumes of water rushing in and great bubbles surging upward towards the light. He beat his arms forward and swerved aside as something appeared below him.

Up from the opening came a glittering silvery mass, shaking with compressed energy, leaping past him, splitting into pair and multiple, trailing small eager miniatures of itself, accompanied by more leaping bubbles and finally in the midst of all, a pastel sphere which sprang for the surface.

Turbulence twisted him and flung him upwards in their wake. Air vomited from his lungs as pressures equalised, and he regained his aqualibrium several feet below the bobbing, searching Guardian which he had apparently set off. It meant he would have to cover at least some of the distance back submerged – he rolled over and blew out through his nose to clear his mask of the water it had shipped during that brief violent rise, and then lifted the face plate just clear of the surface long enough to take a quick orientation from the promontory, then sank, turned and struck out for home. He sank to a cruising depth of five feet, laid his arms back, locked his feet together, kicking rapidly from the knees, rolling his hips and torso in the spine-aching sprint of the dolphin kick. Skip-breathing lightly, he shot north with the sun's warmth faintly perceptible on his back.

He swam thus for two minutes, then surfaced and rolled over to look behind him for the Guardian. It was gone. He cut off his tank valve and spat out the mouthpiece. From here on it was straight Australian crawl for five minutes more.

He flopped into his raft and lay limply in the bottom for several minutes before he stirred. The pressure in the tank was dangerously low, but he had only a minute or two of work to do on the bottom and he might have as much as three minutes of air left. He lashed the wrench to his belt again, adjusted his mask, bit on the mouthpiece and rolled overboard for the last time.

It was becoming an effort to draw air into his lungs by the

time he reached the bottom. He pulled himself down to the smooth stony floor of the lifeless sea and slid under the canted curve of the hull frame with his wrench extended to seek out the three bolts that held the ballast section in place. Since three hundred pounds of petrol and trapped air displaced some four hundred fifty pounds of seawater, the resultant lift would carry his wire-mesh hull aloft nearly as rapidly as his expanding life-rafts.

His chest was beginning to ache with the strain of breathing from the depleted tank. He groped in the dimness for each nut and fumbled the wrench to grip them and turn. The first came out easily, as the frame was still held rigid. But the whole mass shifted microscopically as the second nut gave, and the bolt seemed suddenly fixed in place. He pushed at it with the handle of the wrench, then kicked at the handle to drive it through.

As it popped out, the whole hulk lurched and leaped against the weight of the ballast, which now hung from a single bolt. The nut eased, and the weight followed it down as he backed it off. Bracing his legs against the mass he drew the nut to the last thread, then gave a long sharp twist and pushed himself violently away as the keel dropped and he was sucked upward in a fierce, inverted maelstrom.

His vision blurred and his head was beginning to throb. He crouched and kicked for the surface, shooting upward through green infinities for an endless rush of time until light burst upon him and he gasped in fresh air around the exhausted rubber plug in his mouth before he fell back in the water and stroked feebly for the raft. There he secured a line from the bobbing stern of his hull to a side cleat and collapsed.

Ten minutes' rest restored him sufficiently to attach a tow line and begin paddling for shore. Number 94 was asleep on top of the seawall, knees up, straw hat over his eyes, and no amount of hailing would disturb his slumber. At length, as he neared the shore, Number 6 attracted the attention of an elderly gentleman who was persuaded to prod the napper awake with his cane.

The shell weighed only a fraction as much as the KAR, but it didn't have wheels. The windlass and electric truck were called into service again, and it was 3:30 before Number 6 was able to strip off his wet suit, heat a can of soup, and flop into a warm tub.

No word from Number 2 came to disturb him – two days of backbreaking labour and two months of rebuilding might be expected to serve as his punishment for attempting to escape, but the SCUBA diving had been a thorough threat as well as most informative (in certain negative ways), and the opportunity to put his artificially maintained physical conditioning to use had been exhilarating. And he had come out of the entire exchange with nearly everything he had put into it – plus a number of new questions. If only he could be sure what had happened to his ignition system . . .

Section IV: Rondo Cappriccioso

He had to rearrange his afternoons to include three or four hours shopwork on the restoration of his derelict vehicle; it became his primary occupation. His mornings remained much the same, going about the Village in the streets, cadging pints of petrol from the Chemist's and solvent from the Artist's Shoppe.

Three days after his salvage job, he was sitting alone on the Terrace when a shadow fell across his table and he looked up. Number 18 was studying him uncertainly.

'Are you – uh – feeling sociable?' she asked tentatively.

He wondered what she would do if he stared blankly at her in total non-recognition, or grinned foolishly and began to babble inanities. But it would gain him nothing. So he said, 'Certainly. Why shouldn't I be?' and pushed the other chair out from the table with his foot.

'Well, I'd heard – you'd built a boat, but it sank.' She

shifted her weight doubtfully, eyeing the proffered chair. 'And I hadn't seen you here for lunch for a few days, and I wasn't sure how you were feeling. I mean, you might not want company.'

'I appreciate your concern, but I'm feeling quite well. I've just ordered lunch – we can have the waitress back for you.'

Relieved, she sat down and leaned forward over the table. 'Did you really raise it after it sank? I'd heard you could be seen from the Lookout Tower with a pair of glasses, but I never got a chance to get up there during the day. You were only working in the mornings for a couple of days, weren't you?'

'Yes. I got it ashore all right, but it'll be some time before I can take you for a drive.'

She pouted prettily. 'Oh dear, and I've been so looking forward to seeing your car. Don't you ever allow visitors?'

'Some I can't keep out – Number 2 used to walk right in whenever he felt like it, but that was his inalienable privilege. And speaking of Number 2, who is running things up there now?'

'Number 2, of course. Well, he's still technically Two Prime, pending the hearing.'

'Hearing?'

'It's been postposed until Number 100 is out of the hospital. He's being treated for shock and exposure, and of course they can't hold a hearing until he's in condition to testify.'

'What kind of hearing?'

'Into his desertion, of course. He was apparently running away with the help of one of the guests. Leaving the Village leaderless until Number 2 took responsibility.

'What about Number 3?'

'*What* about Number 3?'

'Number 2 was Number 4 before; why didn't Number 3 become Number 2?'

'Why should she?'

'Because three follows two, as a general rule.'

'Oh, silly! You don't elect your Members of Parliament in alphabetical order. I don't pretend to know what goes on up at the Green Dome, but I presume whatever happened there was some perfectly good reason for it. There's nothing I could do about it either way anyway, even if I cared.'

'So regardless of reasons, Number 2 is effectively in charge of things for the time being.'

'Well, yes! Somebody has to be.'

'Why?'

'Well – because things don't just take care of themselves.'

'Are you ready to order?' The waitress stood, pencil poised, to change the subject. When she had departed, Number 18 showed no interest in returning to local politics.

'I saw you out walking with your cat this morning – through my window. That was why I came here to look for you.'

'I'm flattered. I walk every morning – sometimes the cat follows me. Where's your window? I can wave to you.'

*

The cat had taken to following him on his daily walking tours of the Village. One morning it was scampering ahead of him through one of the leafy lanes that surrounded the Village, and stopped suddenly by a low mint-like shrub.

Number 6 stopped as well, some distance away, to observe the animal's uncharacteristic behaviour.

It sniffed at the dark green leaves, rubbed its nose up against them and bit a piece from one. It backed off, shook its head, and then nosed insistently at the plant again, nipping at the leaves.

Number 6 marked the spot in his mind, and shortly before midnight, on his evening round, he stopped there again for a closer look at the shrub. As a matter of policy, he kept his real interests as covert as possible in the Village. The leaves were small and pointed; he pulled one off, crushed it between his fingers to smell the oil. It was minty, but sweeter; correctly, he identified it as catnip. It might prove useful to have available; he loosened the earth around the root system with his fingers and lifted it, soil and all, into a small paper bag.

He stood, unselfconsciously brushing his knees, slipped the closed sack inside his coat, and continued his evening constitutional. On his return, he came around the workshop at the rear of his cottage. There he knelt again to scrape a small hole in the soft earth of his own flowering border. Gently he slipped the rootlet-laced dirt lump with its leafy crown from the bag and into the hole. He tamped the earth lightly down all around and sprinkled it well with natural nitrates before he went inside.

He seldom thought much about his life outside while he was in the Village. The other world was a place to try and reach – a goal, rather than an urgent detailed reality. But he remembered, in an odd flash of memory, how a girl had offered him a kitten once, years ago when he had first moved to London. She had said he was too lonely for his human good, and needed something else alive around him. But his work had been irregular, even then – he could not afford to keep anything dependent upon his continued existence from one day to another.

The entire memory came back to him in one piece as the black cat stood up on the sofa and stretched, then ambled over to see if his arrival indicated food or attention. Number 6 bent to scratch him behind the ears, then hung his blazer over the back of a chair and sat down at the computer terminal console.

His evenings were now occupied with another design project – one of intricate and exquisite complexity, of the next order of difficulty beyond his late hull, and he had a large amount of study to put in on it. He had taken several books from the Village library on model airplane construction, and had pieced their contents together into complex formulae of lift and drag, centres of gravity, cambers, stresses and loads. Designing something that could maintain an even keel and support itself in midair was by no means as easy as balsa gliders might lead one to expect; he found stimulating challenge in the problem he had posed himself.

The terminal he treated as a toy, and took a simple delight in its usefulness; not only could it accept his sketches, correct them and vary them as he directed, it could print out a reference copy on white paper in seconds on command. Its capabilities were not limited to engineering drawing: he produced a passable sketch of a sleeping cat in two evenings' work, ordered the machine to make three copies, serially numbered in the corner, and erase the picture. One he intended to give to Number 100, if he ever saw him again, and if it would have any reference to him by then – the other he considered for Number 40, Number 18, or Number 61, and decided to postpone a decision.

While he worked patiently at recovering lost ground and forging ahead theoretically, one week followed another. Four of them paced through the Village, carrying summer into autumn while Number 6 continued restoring his engine. It involved a complete disassembly of every moving part, its individual cleaning, drying, inspection and oiling before careful re-assembly. It was a gigantic three-dimensional jigsaw puzzle – a familiar puzzle, about as interesting as building a car from a kit.

He had discovered quite by accident one morning that the cat was likely to chase a ball of crumpled paper if it was thrown near him; it did this with every evidence of enjoyment, and he took to carrying an old tennis ball in the pocket of his blazer when he took his regular walks about the Village. From time to time he would throw it, and the cat would leap after it as if it were a bird. When it landed and bounced and rolled, the animal would wander up to it, sometimes sniff at it, then lose interest. A harmless enough diversion, surely. The cat would never be trained to fetch like a dog, offering slavish devotion in return for attention.

His days blended slowly into one another. Nothing ever changed in the Village but the slow clock of the seasons. Escape was still his goal, but he saw the path clearly ahead of him and was proceeding with all deliberate speed toward his goal. No more particular concentration was needed on the problem. His work progressed automatically from day to day as the KAR gradually grew back together, regenerated by his own two hands – and a wall full of tools.

*

The pieces were nearly together when Number 18 invited him over for dinner one evening and he accepted. Their luncheon conversation, somehow, had turned to fish and devolved to a debate between poached and grilled whitefish. This had led inevitably to her offer and his acceptance.

The butcher had a fresh catch on display, which had inspired the discussion, and his finest and firmest fillet went into her bag with a double handful of chipped ice.

'That's a fine piece of fish you've got there, Number 18. Going to fry it?'

'Oh, no. It's quite fresh enough to poach.'

'That's a delicate flavour for poaching.'

'Poaching can be the gentlest way to cook something light – when it's properly done.'

'I find it a little dry to be grilled,' she added to Number 6 that evening as they resumed their discussion in her quiet cottage unit after dinner. He had to admit he had been well fed, and she had some valid views on the subject of food.

He smiled. 'It takes a good deal of heat to grill properly. If the juices are sealed inside instead of being driven off as steam, it's quite juicy – and less oily than most fish. Why not be my guest tomorrow night? There should be a fresh catch in, and if not, grilling is more forgiving of an extra day in the freezer.'

'Honestly, I thought you'd never ask me. Have you got your car fixed yet? I'd love to come. I heard . . . Is your place really done up exactly like a city flat? With view-windows and all? How exciting!'

'Yes. It was done especially for me with no little trouble and expense, as Number 2 would have been able to tell you at great length.'

'Speaking of Number 100, the hearing was announced this afternoon by the *Village Voice*. It's a month away. They probably want to be sure he's recovered completely.'

'Oh. Is he out of the hospital?'

'I don't know. I don't know whether he's been mentioned recently at all, come to think of it. Would you care for a drink?'

'Gin.'

'Anything with it?'

'Water.'

*

The waning moon was high as Number 6 walked a leisurely, circuitous route homeward. The Village seemed to sleep, with only a few dim lights left on – though the silent traverse of a concealed camera studying an esoteric spectrum might go unobserved, and microphones might lie as silently as sprinkler heads in the grass. The Village was always awake somewhere, watching, listening. And a lone figure passed along the paths, with a faint regular crunch of rubbersoled shoes on gravel.

His steps became silent as he cut across the wide green commons, past the empty flagpole; crunching twice, sharply, on lateral paths, then turning up a narrow lane between two comfortably nestled cottages. The sound of his soft springshod feet padding on cobblestones diminished into the darkness.

The dim glow of a lawn-lamp showed him his own doorstep seventy yards away when suddenly the light was blocked by a figure which stepped out of the bushes ahead of him, and spoke urgently.

'Wait, Number 6! Please –'

The voice was less steady than the last time he had heard it, but there was no mistaking the metallic harshness of Number 100's voice. The raucous quality was still there, but an edge of tension and fear lent it a grotesque quality, like a puppet screaming.

'– I must talk with you!'

'By all means, Number 100! Come inside and we'll talk over plans for our next escape attempt!'

'Number 6, you swine! I never did anything but what was best for you – now that I stand on the brink of extinction, when a word from you could save me, your first words are a shoe planted in the middle of my back! I must talk with you – we must talk alone. We are safe here only for a few minutes – not long enough to explain what's going on and answer half your questions. But I will answer your questions, I swear, if you'll leave me a chance to do anything.'

'Where would we be safe for longer than a few minutes? You should know that better than anyone.'

'Your workshop out at the track. If you'd been anywhere near going out there I'd never have dared come this close to your place.'

'Why is *it* safe?'

'You are the Elephant's Child with your questions! I can't stay. Meet me there tomorrow afternoon. You could have any number of perfectly good reasons for going out there. Make it four o'clock. Be seeing you.' And he was gone.

Number 6 stared after him. After several seconds he shook his head doubtfully and started up the walk again. The Village more than once had reminded him of Dodgson's *Wonderland*, but he didn't think he had ever met the White Rabbit before.

*

At about a quarter to 4:00 the next afternoon he laid down his tools and wiped most of the grease from his hands. He pulled his second blazer on, saving his best to wear for dinner, and made a mental note to stop by the butcher's for the pick of the morning's catch on the way home.

The distant bells of the Village clock were chiming the hour when he arrived at his workshop, and there indeed was Number 100, uncommonly clad in grey overalls and a peaked cap. A metal tray with a grim tin military tea service stood in the corner.

'Ah, Number 6. Punctual to the moment. You must forgive my playing host this time, since I welcome you to your own shop, but do sit down and have a cuppa. The water's just on the boil.'

Momentarily speechless, Number 6 sank to rest on one of the corners of the framework which lay about the shop awaiting some kind of re-assembly. A moment later he found a steaming cup balanced on his knee. He took the saucer gingerly and stood to help himself to the sugar as he spoke.

'You suppose I'm wondering why you called me here.'

'I'm sorry the location isn't more palatial, but I am not exactly a free man at the moment.'

'Ah, which of us is!'

'"No man who lives can be said to be free," after all. But I must confess I did not intend this purely as a social occasion. I arranged this meeting (with no little difficulty) because I must have your help in setting things to rights. Since you are responsible for my being placed in this position, you owe me your assistance in getting out of it. Number 6, you know I've done everything I could to help you while you were here. You owe me at least a little consideration, on that basis alone.'

'Very well – I'll consider you. What else do you want me to do?'

'Help me. My record is stained, my career wrecked because of you! You can help me by telling what happened that – that *awful* night – at the hearing. But if Number 4 thinks he can –'

'You mean Number Two Prime.'

'Number 2 is his own invention. He has taken this excuse to seize executive control of the Village, and is intent on destroying me to assure his position. But several people – some in high places – are aware of what he's trying, and with their help I hope to defeat him and regain the Chair.'

'You talk as if you were autonomous. Doesn't Number One have anything to say about this? Go ahead – I believe you promised something about answering my questions. Do we have enough time to start now?'

'We have nearly an hour.'

'Where am I?'

'In the Village.'

‘Thank you. Where is the Village?’

‘On the western shore of the Balearic Islands. If you were to sail north three hundred miles, you’d hit Barcelona.’

‘Who is Number One?’

‘There is no Number One. The founder and first administrator of the Village was Number One. When he – left us – his Number was retired. Chief administrators since have been Number 2, reminding us that ours is not the supremely dominant power, but the subservient.’

‘Then, in whose name do you administrate? The government – or whatever – behind all this?’

‘In the name of her Royal Majesty, Elizabeth Regina. This is an unofficially unrecognised cranny of the Civil Service. Surely you didn’t think the Mongolians had built and peopled this place!’

‘Who did people it?’

‘Believe it or not, most of these people are here voluntarily. When the Other Side retires their code clerks, they run away to Canada. We offer ours a comfortable, secure resort.’

‘And if they’re not ready to retire?’

‘You are a special case, Number 6. Surely you were aware of that much! You are here for a reason, rather than an excuse. Attend: your precipitous resignation from your – ah – sensitive position came as less than a total surprise to your superiors: you were under scrutiny for some time before you took that step. There had been some evidence of your dissatisfaction with the job you had to do, and you had already been considered for review. Your resignation was regarded as a definite sign of emotional instability –

naturally, you could never have been allowed in the field again under such circumstances.

'But you were still a brilliantly trained man – a valuable expert whose knowledge and talents were still needed by his country. And the Village had an important use for someone of your formidable abilities. Much of our automation is in the experimental stage; all our defences are still being tested. It was, of course, essential that you should remain unaware of the nature of the project in which you were participating so that you would put forth your most sincere efforts towards confounding our systems.'

'I am the Fool you found to determine whether everything was Foolproof.'

'I shouldn't have put it quite so bluntly, Number 6, but you do have a certain turn of phrase there.'

'Let's get more specific. What were you in the hospital for, and why are you free of observation now?'

'Frankly, I was there for Corrective Therapy. But due to the . . . *personal* nature of Number 4's usurpation – and partly out of friendship – a number of the technical staff have remained loyal to me and my cause. With their help I was diverted from most of the treatment Number 2 had me scheduled for. Also, I am able to evade his surveillance from time to time. This workshop is an example. The camera group that covers this area was installed while we were building it – since it was part of my own project, it was regularly monitored by staff who shared my interest in it. Now they remain loyal to me. Number 2 need never know anything that goes on here. We can arrange to signal you should he ever demand to see the coverage of the place and show him instead a videotape of the entire area deserted.'

'And all I have to do for you is . . .?'

'Be my ally. I've spent my life behind a series of desks – you're accustomed to direct conflict and physical confrontation.'

'I've retired.'

'Yes, of course. *Too many people knew too much,* I believe. *Too many people were being killed.* But this is hardly a military operation, Number 6 – murder is not an acceptable part of intra-departmental politics at this level. Only my career is at stake – and perhaps part of my mind.'

'You seem very concerned for my testimony at the hearing.'

'The hearing? That's farce. Number 2 will have rigged it in his own favour; he wouldn't take so great a risk to seize power and then chance losing it on some slight whim of fact. We still have some time before this hearing – it may even be postponed. As long as it is still pending, I can remain in the Village; once I am taken away, I can never return in my old classification.

'Number 2 is only allowing you to continue working on your car because he cannot change my established policies until the hearing confirms him and dissolves the Prime. Because of this, you need make no attempt to disguise your covert activities as long as you do nothing obviously illegal and *demanding* action on his part. But if this hearing goes against me, he will immediately institute his own policies and you will be cut back to a Meccano set. Honestly – haven't I done more for you than Number 2? Is he likely to continue your petrol supply? What would his reaction be to another attempted extension of your track? Do you really expect him to help you obtain replacement parts for those ruined by immersion?'

'Can you? Or is this job payment-on-completion?'

'I can't give you more track or guarantee petrol until I'm back in the Chair. But I can get you some things. I should be able to get whatever parts you may need through my remaining contacts; I've not lost all my influence along with my official position. So you see, we can help each other in many ways. If we succeed, I can promise you immunity for almost anything you do even nominally on my behalf – if we fail, I think you now understand enough about your position here to know that your punishment would perforce be perfunctory.'

Number 6 studied him for several seconds. 'Do you mean you want me to set up a palace revolution for you? A bloodless *coup*?'

'I fear it amounts to that. I have already hopelessly compromised your necessary ignorance of the true situation. The die is cast, the Rubicon crossed, the cat out of the bag and the fat in the fire. I am wholly at your mercy. You could march up to the front door of the Green Dome tomorrow and destroy the entire experiment which is centred around you. Or you can – well, continue as you are. Do your best against our defences. Plan ways of getting past them. Keep working on your machine. In short, act as if you knew nothing. It shouldn't be difficult.'

'Thank you. But since I don't know the way things are put together behind the scenes, you will have to direct me. What specific combination of circumstances could replace you in the Chair?'

'Why . . . I don't really know, exactly. We couldn't do it

with him actually there. *He* had to wait until I was miles outside the Village before he dared.'

'Did he? Or was it only that he needed a legal pretext? Couldn't he have accomplished the same thing if you were, say, out of the room? What if you were on the far side of the Village? What if you were out at the track for half an hour?'

'Why . . . I think it took him nearly an hour to establish complete command. My friends were trying to find me, to contact me, to warn me to take action against him. As Number 2 I could have stopped him with three words. But as Number 100 . . .'

'Would it take you an hour to resume command?'

'I . . . I don't know. If he hasn't destroyed the voice-coded overrides it shouldn't take that long. He was unfamiliar with much of my equipment, which must have delayed him as well . . . Given advance warning for adequate preparation, I could sit in the Chair for ten minutes, free of interruption, and pick up all the threads to a point where he could no longer pose a threat.'

'What is "adequate preparation"?'

'My friends, my associates, would have to be alerted. There is bound to be disconcertment in the Village when the change in administration becomes known, and they can explain the situation directly to anyone who asks, thereby averting any loss of faith in the stability of the Village power structure.'

'You want me to lure him out of the Round Room for ten or fifteen minutes, at some pre-arranged time. How far in advance will you have to know?'

'A day – eighteen hours at least.'

'You know Number 2 far better than I'; what do you think would bring him out of his shell?'

'It shouldn't take much at the moment. Remember, he thinks he has nothing to fear from us. Perhaps if you appeared to be planning some particularly outré device, he might be tempted to come out and take a look at it; what *are* you doing with your hands these days, by the way? Still digging seaweed out of your cylinders?'

'The engine's nearly re-assembled. But your mentioning seaweed reminds me – your fee for my talents includes answers to direct questions, and I have several more.'

'I don't know everything, Number 6. But you are welcome to the answers I have.'

'Why is there no seaweed or any other form of marine life in the Village Bay?'

'Isn't there? How odd!'

'That's why I asked.'

'I'm afraid that's something I don't know anything at all about. I have read of areas of the sea where some freak of current sweeps everything from the face of bedrock and allows nothing to grow. Or perhaps submarine oil seepage sterilised it. The Village was here before I was, Number 6, and I never doubted there were things about it I didn't know.'

'What are the Guardians?'

'This I know, but it may be difficult to explain. Are you at all acquainted with Fluidics?'

'Only vaguely.'

'Fluidics studies the flow of fluids the same way electronics studies the flow of electricity. Fluid flows can be modulated in much the same way as electric current:

amplified, switched off and on with great speed and accuracy – and all, in a properly designed system, with no moving parts. The flow patterns of the fluid medium itself can be made to vary each other in stable, metastable or oscillating states – I don't fully understand it; as I may have mentioned, I'm not at all technically minded. It's analogous to but not at all identical with resistors, capacitors, valves and things in electronics, and there are many applications where fluidic controls are far more efficient than electronic.

'Next, do you know what a Colloidal Mechanism is?'

'Is a Guardian a colloidal mechanism?'

'Not entirely. Please, Number 6, I don't mean to seem to evade your question, but my position is awkward. Suppose a Hottentot attends a Peace Corps school and gets the equivalent of Primary School physical science. When he goes home, he takes a transistor radio with him, and his whole tribe orders him to tell them how it works. You must have patience with me.'

'Do I need to understand the theory behind them?'

'Do you want to? You'd probably best find someone else who could explain it. Or ask your terminal. Perhaps you could simplify your question.'

'Are they alive?'

'Not as we understand life. No.'

'Are they conscious?'

'They are aware, but they have no self-awareness. They are partly self-programming, an advantage fluidics has over electronics, requiring fewer and less delicate transducers to interpret its environment and learn from experience. That's something I know about. Events leave resonant waves in their control systems, and these waves predispose the thing to act in certain ways. When we first receive them, they are as small as soccer balls, and must be programmed to their basic moves in conditioning rooms. They're rather cute when they're small.'

'Then they grow.'

'Oh yes. They are also self-repairing, unless severely damaged. Another advantage of Colloidal Mechanisms. Do you have the time?'

'Half past four.'

'I'd best be getting back. I'll have to take the tea service with me; I borrowed it from the hospital ward-room. You may finish the biscuits – they stale quickly if left out.'

'Where can I deposit a list of replacement parts I want?'

'Prepare three copies and I shall pick them up from you the next time your residence is safe for me.'

'Triplicate?'

'There are three different places – departments – which might have anything you could want. I don't know who would have what. It will be easier if I can give them each a copy than if they have to pass one around. Faster, too, I shouldn't wonder.'

'I must be off – they're expecting me for hydrotherapy at a quarter to. Be seeing you.' Number 100 shouldered the spent tea-tray and departed.

Number 6 rose, picked up his straw hat and the rest of the biscuits and left as well, down a different path, toward the centre of the Village. He had a dinner engagement with a whitefish.

*

Dinner was successful on all counts. His original Hock sauce worked out perfectly, and Number 18 was properly impressed with the entire production. When it was over and the dishes were stacked, she picked up her light coat and said, 'It's such a lovely evening – could you show me your workshop out at the track? I'd love to see it and besides, I think a walk would do us both good after that marvellous dinner.'

They chatted idly for the twenty-minute walk, but once inside the shed her manner changed from flirtatious to conspiratorial. 'Number 100 was to see you today, wasn't he,' she said. 'I do hope you've agreed to help us.'

'To overthrow constituted authority by force and violence?'

'Oh, certainly not! Besides, Number 2 isn't constituted, just *de facto*. And there isn't supposed to be any force or violence, either. If we can just get Number 100 back into his rightful position, there won't even have to *be* a hearing and the status can go back to being quo.'

'Number 100 didn't go into detail about his supporters in the Village, though he gave me to understand they were numerous and ubiquitous. Still, I must admit I never thought of you as a political activist.'

'It isn't a matter of politics, Number 6. I just feel that Number 2 is being unnecessarily high-handed about all this, and is really not justified in punishing Number 100 for what was, after all, mostly your fault.'

'You seem to have learned a lot in the last month – did Number 100 tell you what happened?'

'Well . . . I think he exaggerated some of it. But you were

with him all the time he was away from the Village, even when your boat sank, weren't you?'

'Yes.'

'But you didn't really kidnap him on purpose, did you?'

'No.'

'I couldn't see you going out of your way to take him along in a boat, no matter what he told me.'

'Thank you. Did he mention anything about what happened to the boat's motor? Why it stopped?'

'Stopped? No – just that it sunk while the Rescue Unit was towing you back to the Village.'

'The engine died suddenly, and I believe some outer defence line was responsible. I'd like to know what it is.'

She flushed. 'Really, Number 6 – I'm sorry I brought the matter up. This – this fixation of yours seems to become involved in everything you do. I hope you can suppress it if you intend to help Number 100's cause.'

'Pardon my honesty. I didn't mean to embarrass you.'

'Now about the . . . What is this, exactly? It's not a revolution, or even an underground . . .'

'A counter-coup?' he suggested.

'Anyway, if you want to get in touch with Number 100 bring your message to me at lunch on a sheet of paper in an envelope. I take memos and things from my boss, Number 11, to the Central Kitchen every afternoon. I can meet one of the hospital therapists there and pass it to him, and he can see that Number 100 gets it by six o'clock. Number 100 can usually get out after dark; if he can't, I'll come, because I can get in to see him once a week.'

'How many people are involved in this network? I begin

to get the impression Number 2 stands nearly alone. Why don't you just pull his power points?'

'I guess there must be fifty or a hundred people, inside and outside, who are willing to support us to some extent.'

'How far is that?'

'Well . . . that depends. Some would even be willing to sign a petition. But not enough, I guess. Most of them will help if it doesn't mean going much out of their way and if nobody's likely to find out they're helping. Like carrying notes, and skipping log checks, and passing falsified test reports – if they're well enough falsified. You know, that sort of thing.'

'I know that sort of thing.' He stood up. 'I'll want to make out a list for you to deliver to Number 100 through your "underground." I can give it to you over lunch tomorrow.'

'By the way,' she asked, pointing, 'are those big metal things all that's left of your boat?'

'That's all there was of the boat – except for the car.'

'Oh . . . Wasn't it kind of small?'

'It did well enough – as far as it went.'

'As far as it . . . Number 6, I wish you would control your gift for innuendo – isn't any subject safe from you?'

'You asked about my boat – weren't you aware of its purpose?'

'Well . . . I just don't like to think about it. I admire it as a boat – I don't know anything about what else you may have done with it, and please don't tell me.'

'You don't object to the boat – you only object to its being used as a boat.'

'No – not exactly. I mean . . . a boat is a nice thing. It just shouldn't be used for . . . *anti-social* purposes.'

'If you will pardon my crudity, why would my departure – *alone* – have been anti-social?'

'Well, because you are rejecting society! Anti-social means against society. And if you want to get away from us, reject us, that's against our society.'

'But I'm not doing anything *to* your society.'

'Yes, you are – you're rejecting us.'

'It is my right to reject it.'

'No, it isn't! You can't live outside of society. Not and remain human.'

'There is the kernel of our disagreement. I wish Number 100 were here to demonstrate his Famous Mathematical Proof that there is no such thing as an individual except as a reference unit in statistical aggregations.'

'What? I don't really understand statistics.'

'Never mind. He said the same thing you did with more numbers and less emotion, and took ten times as long to say it. As your host I apologise for this disagreement of opinion, but I beg the right to maintain my own.'

'But it's *wrong*!'

'I also have the right to be wrong.'

'But why do you want to be wrong?'

Number 6 sat down. He regretted the turn the conversation had taken, but refused to default. 'I don't *intend* to be wrong,' he said patiently. 'But I want to be able to make my own mistakes and learn from them.'

She stared at him. 'And if somebody saw you were making a mistake, you wouldn't want them to stop you.'

'Essentially.'

She shook her head slowly, keeping her eyes fixed on his face, and chewed her lower lip in sincere confusion. 'I'm afraid I don't understand you, Number 6.'

'I'm afraid you do. Perhaps we'd better get back to the boat. Or perhaps, considering the hour, we'd best be getting back home.'

'Well . . .'

'I'll take you for a drive when I have the KAR running again.'

'Then you will help us.'

Number 6 shrugged. 'I'll cooperate in return for certain concessions,' he said. 'Such as replacement parts. I'll bring you an itemised list for lunch tomorrow.'

'It sounds unappetising after your dinner tonight,' she said with a tentative smile.

'Thank you,' he said, rising to his feet and extending his hand. 'Shall we toddle back to my place for dessert?'

'Just a bit – I have my work to do tomorrow.'

'And mine.'

*

The requisition he drew up for Number 100 to put into his channels was the subject of much thought and intensive calculation. Only certain items of the highest priority were called for. Most, but not all, of them would incidentally be essential to his most recently revised private plans, a fact which he chose not to bring to his benefactor's attention.

As it was, it ran to six pages in three copies, with detailed specifications on several entries. Number 18 frowned when he passed the bundle to her under the table on the Terrace.

'I offered to smuggle him notes,' she murmured. 'Not the *Encyclopedia Britannica.* I hope this will fit in my folder.'

'I should have written smaller. Could you supply me with a microfilm camera?

'Shh. The waitress cannot be trusted.'

'Sorry.'

*

The following afternoon, when he unwrapped a beautiful hock of ham Number 61 had carved for him, he found a note stuck to the side of it. The paper was translucent with absorbed fat, and heavy pencilled block letters were almost legible through it. He peeled it off with a bemused smile and wiped the faint black smears of graphite from the tough, slick rind.

SAME PLACE. 9 P.M.

He wondered if he were expected to devour the note once he had memorised its contents. Number 100 must have some purpose behind this charade; perhaps he could be persuaded to offer an explanation this evening.

*

'Why this amateur underground of yours? You gave me the impression my testimony at the hearing would set things legally to rights.'

'Frankly, Number 6, I hadn't told you this because I wasn't entirely sure how far Number 4 – Number 2 I should say – had got in his mad clutch at power. But it now seems extremely doubtful that your testimony would even be admissible at the hearing. You would be held in the position of co-defendant of the second order, whereby you would be presumed to be pleading your own case in such testimony. Number 15 explained it to me last week.'

Number 100 was clad in the ice-cream uniform of the Village Neatness Committee; it was one size too large for him and lent the shards of his raucous arrogance a certain bedraggled dignity. He paced nervously back and forth across the closed end of the workshop.

'But even without your testimony, you are the only man who can help me regain my proper position. Let me explain to you what we have in mind. Somehow or other I must get from the hospital up to the Round Room while you devise some way of distracting Number 2 from his position there.'

'How long will it take you to cover the distance?'

'Why, I don't know. It depends on how, and when, and how soon.'

'Fine. You know the Village backstage better than I; why don't *you* determine a time, based on when you'll be ready, and let me know. Since I'm working alone, I can prepare a sufficiently attractive distraction on relatively short notice.'

'How much notice?'

'Eighteen hours – a day at most.'

'That will do nicely. I really daren't stay much longer or they'll be looking for me. Some time in the next day or two we should be ready to move – I'll send you word.'

'What if I don't happen to stop by the butcher's for two or three days?'

'Oh, something will turn up, Number 6. My people are everywhere.'

'I don't doubt it.'

'One other minor thing – that list of materials and parts you sent through yesterday seemed a good bit more extensive than your automotive repairs would warrant. You aren't planning to try to leave us again, are you?'

'Would you believe me if I denied it?'

Number 100 sighed and leaned against a rough bench. 'Candidly, no. But if you would only agree to wait a few more days, I shall be back in the Chair. When matters are set right, you may find your status in the Village changed favourably.'

'I'm quite satisfied with my present position.'

'But you're wasting yourself. You are a rare and infinitely valuable man. Most men have the souls of slaves – perhaps they could be said to have voluntarily surrendered their souls. They lack whatever elemental drive, or awareness, or other quality is supposed to make man more than a reasoning animal. It is best for most people that they be . . . taken care of. Tended. Guided. Told what to think and feel. Generally they seem to prefer it that way, you know. Certainly it's easier than having to make up your own mind and take all your own responsibilities. It's so much simpler and more practical to share out responsibilities and decisions.

'*Man* is a collective noun. His greatest strength is in union, in cooperation, in Society. Submerging his own will and his whole being in the greater whole.'

'But *men* are singular. And some of them will take pains to remind you of that fact.'

'Individuality is a valuable talent, Number 6. But so few people actually have it – and so many think they do. You have it, Number 6. You have defended your individuality with the greatest of brilliance and exquisite courage and faith in yourself. You have proved you have what the poet called "that spark of fire divine." Don't divert it to disorder, destruction, disorganisation and chaos. Man's purpose in the universe is to bring order out of chaos. Help us here in the infinitesimal portion of the great task we are attempting.'

'Odd how we can never seem to agree, Number 100. I had always felt the universe was already in pretty good order. It seems to tick along quite nicely without our attention. How do you suppose the Andromeda Galaxy has managed to hold together all these years?'

'"Lift not your hands to it for help, for it as impotently moves as you or I,"' Number 100 quoted mournfully, if obscurely. 'The universe I was referring to, on a practical level, is the universe that pipes in your water and keeps your lights burning, that delivers your milk and distils your precious petrol, that slaughters your meat and mixes medicines and paves roads for you to drive on. The social universe, Number 6. You may be reluctant to admit it, but it supports you and makes your way of life possible.'

'And denies me the right to enjoy it.'

'It does not deny your right – only limits it for the common good. Order induces uniformity where it does not find it, but rejecting the order of society as you do involves your rejection of the foundations of human civilisation.'

'I don't reject civilisation out of hand; it has a number of redeeming features. But I will not have it thrust upon me – nor will I thrust it forceably upon others.'

'And what if they come to you and beg you for it? Come, Number 6 – your collapsible cast-iron kayak isn't remotely ready for another attempt. We shall have adequate time to debate Social Psychology next week, when all this nonsense has been settled.

'Heavens, it's late. I must be getting back. I shall do what I can towards your requests, of course – but what on earth did you want all that sealed nylon fabric for?'

'I wanted it to be a surprise.'

'Oh, very well, Watch for word, and be ready. And in the meantime, do try to behave yourself. Be seeing you.'

The Village bell sent a single gentle chime over the silent woods, and Number 100 was gone into the darkness.

Section V: Scherzo

Two days passed without a word. On the third day, when Number 6 made his regular call on the Village Butcher's Shop, a stranger wore the apron behind the counter.

'Good morning, Number 6. What would you like today?'

'That's a nice set of chops, there. Is Number 61 on holiday?'

'Number 61 was taken very ill last night. The doctors said he might not be back for some time. I've no idea what it was, but apparently it came on very suddenly. I didn't see him, of course. Well, I hope to serve you as well as he did. Here are your chops – will there be anything else?'

'I think not. Be seeing you.'

'And you.'

*

Ninety minutes later Number 18 joined him at their table on the Terrace, her face forcedly bright and cheerful. Under her breath she greeted him with, 'Things are in a mess. Number 61 was picked up last night. Apparently someone let too much slip.'

'Have you any idea who?'

'Well, I have my suspicions. I don't think it was anybody you know. Number 100 called me at the office just half an hour ago and told me to tell you not to worry about this little setback, and that he would get in touch with you. And he also said to be sure to explain that this will be purely a disciplinary problem with which he could deal on the executive level, and he emphasised that you would "not be called upon to rub anybody out," were the words he used.'

'I see.'

'And he said your order would not be held up by this incident and you should start getting things tomorrow or the next day.'

*

It took another month before everything had arrived. Items came in various guises from week to week, and the KAR grew back together a piece at a time. Something was different about the ignition system – something which could not be observed without much closer inspection than a single remote camera afforded: now every lead from the distributor to each spark plug was of heavier cable – shielded cable, grounded inconspicuously to the frame.

It was observed in certain private places that Number 6 had taken up another of his apparently endless hobbies –

sewing. What he might be making from fifteen square yards of heavy sealed nylon fabric was a matter for some professional speculation, but whatever it might be it seemed to grow larger and more complex every day.

Analysis of his computer time use suggested a crude biplane, and the possibility of a gas or hot-air balloon was considered seriously, but the question of what would fill it remained unanswered.

Meanwhile, the subject of this scrutiny cobbled together a new sort of structure from the bare framework of the old – gone was any pretext at a racing silhouette; it began to resemble a free-form sculpture with smoothly polished curves, jagged edges and ends filed, sanded and dotted here and there with dabs of soft solder – narrow curved ribs, broad-bellied in the middle.

Number 100 was conspicuous by his intermittence. Conspiracies were murmured under awnings with a few merchants and Villagers, though nothing ever seemed to come of them. Number 6 wondered from time to time at Number 100's melodramatic inventiveness, but was offered nothing specific to divert him from his regular daily rounds of the Village and meetings with his acquaintances at band concerts and for luncheons on the Terraces as the days grew warmer and summer began to bloom.

Finally his work drew to its conclusion. And one afternoon when the engine ran smoothly and the wheels rolled, Number 18 came back with him from lunch. Number 213 met them at the workshop and led them out to the track, proudly waving his red flag. Unexpectedly, they were met by a five-man welcoming committee, led by Number 11, a blandly personable cipher in his mid-forties.

'I gave my office the afternoon off,' he explained cheerfully. 'Number 18 expected you would be ready today, and we thought a small celebration would be in order. Number 100 should be here any moment – he was especially anxious to see that your automobile was running properly again.'

'Yes, indeed,' said the familiar raucous voice outside the shed as Number 100 entered. 'I saw it as I came up. It seemed to be running nicely.'

He was dressed in an ecstatic purple blazer with gold piping, and Number 94 dismounted from the silent electric cart behind him with champagne and glasses. 'I was hoping to have all this ready when you arrived, Number 6, but circumstances forbade. Still, better late than never.'

Number 94 and Number 11 handed glasses around, splashing a moderate amount of champagne in each; when they had poured for themselves Number 100 raised his glass.

'The lost has been saved,' he announced. 'By strength of purpose and unstinting labour, with a good deal of spare time, Number 6 has won back to the level at which he started. I must admit I never thought you'd do it,' he added. 'Though I myself don't know much about mechanical things, I'd always thought salt water was absolutely fatal to engines.'

'It is. And I'm ahead of where I started – look at the screenwork I have.'

'So I've heard; I'd like to see it. Have you thought of doing it up on a base for entry in the Village Summer Art Festival?'

'Never seriously. I tried that once – didn't especially like it.'

'Oh, come, Number 6! Surely you should be gratified that others found your work enjoyable. Though as I recall you offered the award to another entrant – I forget her Number.' He raised his glass again. 'But let the dead past bury its dead . . . figuratively speaking, of course. I propose a toast to Number 6's success.'

'Past or future?' Number 6 asked as they drank.

'Present. The past is problematical, the future hypothetical. Nevertheless may I propose a second toast – somewhat presumptuously worded, but not, I think, unduly: *to our future success*.'

All eyes on him over a ring of rims, Number 6 joined them. As he held out his glass with the others, he asked, *sotto voce*, 'Will I be expected to make a speech?'

Number 100 ignored him. 'The day after tomorrow will bring at last the confluence of schedules which will make our operation practicable.' He motioned the four strangers Number 6 had observed forward for introductions. 'These men represent personnel interested in this operation – they're the only ones able to get away from their jobs at this time of day, and they will advise anyone else who needs to know of our plans.

'Unless you have thought of an excellent diversion to draw Number 2 from his perch, we have developed an alternative plan. Instead of trying to lure him away, we could achieve the same ends by driving him out. If something like a smoke bomb went off in the Round Room, and two Service Engineers ordered the Room evacuated, Number 2 would go wherever he was told. I could be waiting in the wings, as I believe you phrased it once, and simply step in and pick up the reins where I left them on that ill-considered journey to the seashore in concern for your welfare.'

'It sounds like a reasonable plan,' Number 6 said noncommittally.

'Ah. Praise from a professional. There is, however, a technical problem. What might be termed a "hang-up."'

'There always is.'

'I should suppose so – it's awfully difficult when you've never done this sort of thing before.'

'The smoke bomb.'

'Ah – yes.'

'You want me to build you one.'

'Oh, no. That is quite a commonplace item. The difficulty is in its delivery.'

'And you are here to invite me to beard the the lion and bell the cat.'

'It should be in your province. The way can be cleared for you of human observers, but there are certain securities which cannot be disarmed except from the Chair.'

'I expect you have a diagram?'

'We have a map with notes. You will have to go in tomorrow night after midnight; but it shouldn't take you more than fifteen minutes – it daren't take you more than thirty. I can tell you where to hide it and how to set the timing mechanism. The delay will be twelve hours; if you and Number 18 are on the Terrace as usual, you may observe some consternation up on the Hill at that time. I trust you will show the same amount of detached concern as those around you.'

Number 18 was delighted. 'Then we don't have to do anything when it actually happens?'

'You may applaud quietly. Number 6, I will call on you tomorrow afternoon to discuss your exact schedule of movements and bring you the infernal machine. Now I propose we return to the business at hand: Number 6, your car is ready to run, and we are here to share this triumphant achievement with you as you take your first drive around the track.'

'I'm afraid I can't fit you all in.'

'Vicariously, Number 6, vicariously. Though there *is* space for one passenger . . .'

'Oh, Number 6, you promised me,' said Number 18. 'And I'd be very happy to share it with you.'

They crowded out to the car, and willing hands helped Number 18 to the left-hand seat as Number 6 slid behind the controls. The engine caught at the first touch of the electric starter, and the others stepped briskly back to a respectful distance.

He slipped the transmission into gear, then depressed the foot throttle as he let the clutch in. KAR 1260 moved gracefully forward, accelerating around the corner of the building on to the track. Behind the muffled exhaust, Number 100's voice could be heard leading the others.

'Hip-hip-*hoorah!* Hip-hip-*hoorah!* Hip-hip-*hoorah!*'

The projected Secret Route of Entry was comparatively simple, involving no laundry chutes, air vents or fire escapes – one side door would be opened for him on the last stroke of midnight, and a certain sequence of corridors would be safe for certain periods of time. There were also, of course, a number of specifically defined hazards in the form of detection devices.

Number 100 insisted on taking the plans back with him, and Number 6 was obliged to commit them to memory during the remainder of the afternoon. The smoke bomb was a cylinder about the size of an old fountain pen; it was armed and set by twisting the two halves clockwise to a stop. When it was operating, a blue band would show on its grey plastic surface. When it went off, clouds of black electrical-smelling smoke would billow forth in profusion accompanied by a 13-Hz infrasonic for five minutes. The firing mechanism, he was told, was accurate to within five seconds over a twelve-hour period.

It was nestled in the breast pocket of his black blazer as he strolled late that night near a small green door, half hidden by ivy, off an unfrequented path on the south, or downhill, side of the Green Dome. As the twelfth stroke of the tower clock dropped into the gloom, a blade of greenish-white fluorescent light stood and widened, and he hurried forward to enter the long empty hall opened to him, deserted but for himself and one of the four men who had attended Number 100's recent fete. This anomial worthy greeted him with a forefinger raised to his lips and a terse whisper.

'That door is now locked. You can open it from the inside when you're through. Give it a good push when you go out, to make sure it's closed. I think you know the way from here.'

Number 6 nodded. Straight ahead to the fifth pair of double doors, rubber gloves for the handles. Through the doors to the first elevator bay. The bay monitor would be distracted from 12:02 to 12:04, and the monitor from 12:15 on was One of Us.

He checked his wristwatch and wondered just how much of this charade was for real. If he walked into the lift bay thirty seconds early, would the bluff be called and Number 100's real control revealed? Probably not. There would be great opportunity for tocsins and alarums in the night and all sorts of running about and shouting, which would delight his theatrical heart; but this game board might be armed. The question was perversely tempting, but someone might get hurt in the confusion. Besides, the pressures lent a semblance of reality to his role.

Not for the first time he wondered if he would get enough out of this escapade to make up for the sleep it would cost him. A chance to get into the basement of the Green Dome was not that lightly passed by since the new administration had sealed things over – Number 6's innate curiosity had incited him to inspect the weak points with which he had been familiar and he had found them uniformly reinforced.

Even if Number 100 were being completely honest with him, pains would doubtless be taken to keep him shunted away from anything really interesting. He gave the bay monitor thirty seconds margin, then walked casually across the open space before the cold eye of the camera and stepped through an unlocked door into a vertical-access stairwell. It would remain unlocked until half past twelve.

Up three flights to another door which should have been unlocked at 12:05; he laid his ear to the crack and listened for a full minute before easing it open. The curved hall was deserted. He let the door close silently behind him and lay down on his stomach.

Cautiously he crawled under the invisible beam which crossed the corridor thirty inches from the floor, then rose to his feet, dusted the front of his trousers and blazer, and continued around the curve. Fifty paces took him ninety degrees, and there another of Number 100's ubiquitous friends sat, his feet up on a small desk with a tiny TV screen, a double row of buttons and a side-hung handset. He looked up as Number 6 passed him and nodded recognition, gave him an amiable salute and returned to his magazine.

Twenty paces beyond him a door opening inward stood invitingly ajar as his instructions had promised. Through the gap he saw darkness intermittently lit from flickering display units; the spherical silhouette in the centre was the vacant Chair. With feline silence he moved along the curved wall. Diagonally from him, dimly spotlit like a deserted stage set, a ramp and double doors led out to the foyer. And beside him now, the Ordinary, its penny-farthing wheels and awnings an outré dissonance amid the glittering steel and shifting coloured patterns, like a balloon in a museum. Why was it the symbol of the Village? he wondered. Why did flags, buttons, stationery, mastheads show it? He must remember to ask Number 100 and see how believable his answer was.

The base of the stand that held the antique bicycle erect was high enough and deep enough to hold the grey cylinder; Number 6 took it from his pocket and consulted his wrist chronometer. 12:14:25. He took just half a minute for a piercing look around the room, then watched the second hand snip off the last five seconds. At precisely 12:15 he gave the cylinder a firm twist and felt something click into place; looking closely in the unsteady light he saw the blue band which meant it was armed. He set it gently in place and stepped back to study it critically.

As he did, the room brightened. He looked around quickly to see lights coming up on the main doors and the Chair. It no longer seemed like the time for an extended investigation – he withdrew as gracefully and silently as he had come.

Out in the hall the guard looked up inquiringly as he came past, and Number 6 held up his right hand, thumb and forefinger tip to tip, other fingers extended. The guard smiled, nodded, and returned to his magazine.

Number 6 squirmed gracelessly under the electric eye beam. As he did so, tensing for alarms but curious enough to take the risk, he carefully raised himself on his knees as he crawled through high enough to break the beam. It would look accidental and unconscious from any angle.

The silence remained unbroken. Without pausing, he gained the access stairs and looked up them. He could afford a moment to try . . . Two at a time, he took the next flight up. The door was immovable. He had eight minutes until the door on the ground level would be locked – time enough to check every door from the top of the stairs at the end of the second flight up to the lowest level four flights down from his entrance. The bottom one was not locked.

Beyond the door lay darkness. Cool white light from the stairwell spilled across a cracked concrete floor, stained with seepage and cellardamp; a musty smell wafted out in exchange. On the edge of visibility two or three large dark shadows stood farther back in the unguessable extent of the room.

Number 6's hand felt lightly along the wall for an electric switch, and met nothing but a wisp of spider-web. He looked at his watch again – 12:26:40. Just over three minutes to climb fifty feet. He didn't especially look forward to meeting whoever would be coming to lock the stairwell again, and two minutes in total darkness would be worth little. He released the door and scaled the stairs.

He came out into the familiar elevator bay, tossed an ironic salute to the glassy eye of the camera, and passed through into the hall. He had not removed his rubber gloves since coming in; now he swiftly tried every other door in the long silent hallway. All resisted his touch but one – and that was the last he tried, for it was the door he had come in by and when he pushed it solidly closed behind him; he was outside and there was nothing left to do but go home.

A small black shape extruded itself from the bushes as he came out and the cat wandered up to rub against his leg. He unpocketed the ratty tennis ball he'd carried for his evening walk and tossed it down the homeward path; the cat bounded after it, happy with the pretended quarry. Number 6 smiled wryly and followed the cat at a leisurely pace into the night.

*

He joined Number 18 on the Terrace shortly past noon and ordered a light lunch. When the waitress had gone, she leaned across the round white table and eagerly asked, 'What time does the balloon go up?'

He looked at her with quizzically canted eyebrows. 'Odd

you should choose that expression,' he said. 'A quarter past, give or take five seconds.'

'How long do we have?'

'Another four minutes.'

'Did you have any trouble?'

'Not a bit.'

There were all sorts of plausible reasons why there had been no response to his single unprogrammed departure from assigned precautions, but the most likely under the circumstances still seemed to be some degree of duplicity on the part of Number 100. Now as the time approached for his planted device to function, he sat facing the sea, one eye on his watch and one ear focused behind him.

'What will happen when it goes off? What'll we see?'

'It will make a lot of smoke and some noise, but not likely anything we can see from here. Presumably Number 2′ will dash in a panic to safety, and the Village Fire Brigade will be summoned. That will probably be all we will see – or hear.'

'Now how soon?'

'About a minute.'

Number 18 sat, staring fixedly over his shoulder at the Green Dome as he attacked his watercress sandwich, pausing between segments to call off for her benefit, 'Five-four-three-two-one-pop! Now to see how efficient the Brigade is on a top-priority call.'

He finished his sandwich and picked up his steaming cup of tea. Long moments passed as he stared mistily out to the distant uncertain line where sea and sky ran together, and heard the peaceful sounds of Village life continue undisturbed behind him. Number 18's whisper broke his unconsciously growing tension at last.

'How long has it been?'

He looked at his watch and was faintly startled. 'Five and a half minutes.'

'Nothing's happened. Could it have misfired?'

Number 6 shook his head. 'I have no idea. Number 100 gave me to understand it was a simple foolproof mechanism, and checked me out on its simple foolproof operation. It's quite possible anything could have gone wrong with it – or it could have been found and removed or disarmed. It may show up in my bed tonight. I suggest you ask Number 100. He'll have an answer – he always does.'

*

He didn't. He had no idea what had happened – if anything had been suspected, it could have incited a complete search of the Round Room. And the device had not been undetectably concealed. A pity, but nothing could be done now. It would be best to wait a bit longer before trying anything else – if the bomb had been found, their entire group could be threatened.

For the next two weeks, the only communication between Number 6 and Number 100 was relayed messages carried by Number 18. His working hours centred more around the redesigned framework aluminium bracing and re-formed layers of wire mesh. Now in three sections, two light and one sturdy, it did resemble blunt wings and a platform as large as the car. Only the wings were covered with fine mesh; the open bracing of the small box would open out to a platform with crossbraces locked in place. Intricate and ambivalent as it was, it certainly didn't look as if it would fly.

His sewing project, the sealed nylon fabric, lay apparently forgotten in a heap in the corner of his shop. The cat often curled up there to doze away the warm afternoons of fading summer while its host tinkered and banged happily at whatever monkey-puzzle he was building.

Number 100 appeared around the corner of his shed one such afternoon with his customary unexpectedness, looked around disapprovingly and said, 'Still bent on leaving us, I see.'

'I'll thank you to watch your language in my shop, Number 100. What's new with the Underground?'

'They've opened a Southern Extension with twenty trains an hour. Commuting from Bromley is much easier now. But that's not why I called, as you may have guessed – I thought you might like to know what happened to your infernal machine.'

'The smoke bomb?'

'Apparently it was found by the cleaners and thrown with the morning's trash. And that, of course, was incinerated at dawn. So there was never any suspicion. We could do it again, an hour later to miss the cleaners, and there's no reason why the entire operation couldn't succeed the second time through. Consider the other a dress rehearsal.'

'When did you have in mind?'

'We'll have to resynchronize schedules with a Zero Time of one A.M. Certainly within a week – the next two or three days if we're lucky.'

'And you want me to repeat my previous performance?'

'Precisely. It was *such* a fine job last time – pity the thing attracted the cleaners' attention. They must have come in just as you left. A good thing you didn't meet them! Well, I can't stay – I'll send you your bomb by Number 18 along with instructions on day and timing, since I likely can't get away to wish you luck. I must be going – I have an appointment with a remarkably lovely therapist.' He smirked roguishly, and was gone.

Number 6 had carefully, in fact rather pointedly, refrained from saying anything that could have been construed as acceptance of his visitor's proposal. In the privacy of his own mind he held deeper commitments to other schedules for the next few days.

*

He passed the next two sunsets studying wind currents over the cliffs north of the Village. A seagull would zoom in, wings rigid, folded yellow feet nearly brushing the waves, then bank suddenly into a tight spiral and climb the jutting seaward face. His observations did not pass unobserved, as he expected, and comments were made upon them in high places.

'He's out watching the birds again.'

'You don't actually expect him to try to fly that thing!'

'I expect him to try. There'll be a Rescue Unit right under him with a net. And I don't believe he's seen the Flying Guardians – imagine his surprise when we send them up a mile inland.'

'You've mastered their direction?'

'They're helpless against a ten-knot breeze, but Number

6 will need fairly still air for his daring ascent, and once aloft he must fly before the wind.'

'Suppose he needn't? If he can fill a gas bag he can power an airscrew.'

'Reinforcement of one area does not weaken another. Number 6 will not pass our outermost border.'

'You're confident.'

'This is the Village.'

*

Three nights later, when the moon was at quarter, he had not heard again from Number 100. Towards dusk he loaded his KAR 1260 for a drive down to the shore. The black cat, like a mascot, leaped into the passenger seat at his invitation and rode with him to the foot of the track.

The sun on the horizon was a football of gold which dazzled the eye. It squatted there at the end of a broad shimmering highway across the waves, and Number 6 permitted himself a smile at the thought of the open road that waited for him.

Quickly and efficiently, as though he had assembled it many times before, he went through the steps of surrounding the bracing with the shaped and watertight fabric like fitting a slipcover. As he did so, his alert senses caught the incoherent whuffling roar of a Guardian behind him. He turned to see it rolling down the beach toward him, accelerating into a wabbling charge.

Number 6's hand ducked into his pocket and produced the cat's old tennis ball. Clicking his tongue to attract the animal's attention, he let the cat sniff the ball for a moment, then tossed it in a long underarm to the landward side of the approaching Guardian. The cat sprang from the car and darted across the sands after its toy. As the furry shape shot past, the Guardian swerved and veered to follow it.

Immediate danger of interference diverted, Number 6 quickly bolted the open framework between two parallel pontoons and pushed the structure forward into the surf.

His engine caught at the first touch of the starter. He let in the bottom gear and eased KAR forward on to the structure. It settled lower, bobbing unsteadily until he reached the balance point. Then he shifted back into neutral, set the brake and hopped over the door. Balancing on the starboard pontoon, he bent to slip a rubber belt over the rear wheel. Then back into the car, and he erected the aluminium mast, braced between the seats. Shaking out the neatly rolled sail of nylon fabric, it was a matter of moments to snake a heavy cord through eyelets along one edge and line it up along the boom.

The ungainly catamaran rig was lifted now by the risen tide, and as he fed power to the rear wheels he felt the vibrations of the engine and the thrashing of the power screw push him away from the shore. Glancing over his shoulder, he saw the Guardian rolling about the beach in a widening search pattern as though it had lost him entirely.

Before him the last bright line of the sun was vanishing, and Mercury stood bright above it like a yellow beacon. His craft steadied as he drew past the gentle surf to deeper water, and he sped the screw until his engine was ticking at a comfortable three thousand rpm. then he set the rudder and clambered over the body of the KAR to run a quick inspection for stowaways. He was alone.

Already he was past the rocky point where Number 100 had shown himself – now he was approaching the area where his engine had died so mysteriously those many hard-won months ago.

His theories now would be vindicated or he would once again be returned to his Lifelike Habitat. It seemed whatever had affected his car had struck through the ignition, and he suspected the cause. Early in the Second World War there had been a device capable of stopping an internal combustion engine by radio-frequency induction – but the same shielding which prevented ignition systems from interfering with radio communications shielded them from induction as well and it was never used as a weapon. If the Village now were using a related method, his carefully shielded ignition should immunise him against it and at the very least give him a look at their next line of restriction.

The darkening coastline, rugged and sparsely wooded, drifted slowly past a mile away in unreal perspective for many minutes, and still the engine throbbed on. He estimated his speed at a comfortable ten knots – he held it while the sky darkened and the stars appeared. Mercury was gone below the horizon to port before the Great Bear became visible and directed his gaze to Polaris, halfway up the purpling infinite dome of the sky.

Now he steered away from land and raised his sail. As it filled with the seaward breeze he disengaged the engine and switched it off. He trimmed the sail manually until it was as taut as the following wind would make it, and secured its lines.

Again he set the rudder, and rode west with the breeze. The near-quarter moon shone high to his left, and ahead the fading glow of the sunset summoned him. In less than an hour he was out of sight of land.

The breeze held steady for another hour, until the last western glow was extinguished beneath the great dark sea, and a confusion of stars dusted the velvet blackness of the night. At length he brought his sail and rudder about in smooth coordination until he had the prow centred beneath the Northern Star. Then he fixed his sail again, lashed the rudder, and set about one last thorough checkout of everything.

Both pontoons now floated half-filled with gasoline; beneath the seat and packed in the boot of his KAR were bottles of water and cans of food, fishhooks, ropes and the usual gear for extended survival on the open ocean. He no more believed Number 100's statement that they were in the Balearic Islands than he believed his old superiors had been suspicious of his sanity before he'd resigned. He smiled. What a strange set of games Number 100 – if he had ever not been Number 2 – had chosen to play. And how fortunate for *him* that he had been willing to offer real stakes.

Watching the foam fleeing past him in the faintly moon-silvered darkness, he estimated that the continuing breeze now bore him north at a brisk twelve or fifteen knots. The hiss and slap of the bow waves was the only sound in the midst of a silence as vast as the night and the sea. All around him the infinitely distant circle of horizon continued unbroken, and the constellations in their circling courses gave him his steadfast direction to the north.

The running swell of falling tide would carry him further seaward, but the wind should hold until morning. Then he would have to find what wind he could or make do with the engine. At least the skies were clear. Lulled at last by the silence, the release of months of accumulated tensions and a vast sense of accomplishment, he drifted thus in and out of a watchful sleep for some hours.

The first time he woke, the moon had set and Mars was low in the west. The sky seemed paler, somehow, though it was scarcely midnight – he looked up at the stars which no longer seemed to throng uncountably in the black of the sky and realised a thin curtain of mist had been drawn across them.

When he woke again an hour later it was gone, and the Great Bear stood on its head in the west, every star as crisp and sharp as pinholes in black paper. And eventually, Number 6 slept, half-stretched across the cushioned leather seat of his boat, uncomfortably wrapped under the steering wheel, a heavy beach blanket over him to ward off the damp chill of the night.

He didn't waken until the morning sun was bright through the clearing haze. Then he sat stiffly erect, rubbing his eyes.

Ahead of him a dark area on the horizon looked like land. Could it be the coast of Spain? Could Number 100 have been telling the truth? He squinted through the clearing mists of morning towards the dim uncertain shore.

The wind had failed sometime around dawn, and his sails hung limp in the faint movement of air that remained; now he struck the sail and started his engine again. As the machine warmed up he freed the rudder, let in the clutch and speeded the screw.

The distant blue haze resolved. He saw boats on the

water, a town above the beach – small stone houses among trees, nestled between two rocky promontories. He couldn't see more, squinting into the newly risen sun.

As he drew nearer, the light dazzled him. But beneath it, on the rising ground above the small buildings like a watchful mother hen over her brood, stood a Green Dome. And the boats, he could tell, were coming out to meet him.

He put about, knowing he couldn't hope to outdistance forty-knot power launches, and found a pair of twelve-foot spheres floating lightly on the water to seaward of him. His pointed ram was still ready – lifting it to position he gunned the engine towards the nearer Guardian, and without more than a moment of surprise felt the throbbing of the motor cease beneath him.

One sphere spoke with the raucous voice of Number 100, hugely amplified and resonant. 'I'm afraid, Number 6, that you simply cannot be trusted with tools. And after all we've meant to each other. I found the sketch of the cat you made for me – I shall treasure it always. But you must come back – give us another chance.'

'Another chance?'

'To make you feel at home here. We only want you to be happy, Number 6 – and we want you to know that wherever you go, we will always be waiting to welcome you back. I do hope you have had a pleasant sail, though. Be seeing you.'

And by then the boats were around him and hands were reaching down from them to help him aboard.